RARE BIRD
LOS ANGELES, CALIF.

Story and characters created by DAN HOURIHAN,
SPENCER CHARNAS, and ANDREW JUSTIN SMITH

Ice Nine Kills

# The Silver Scream

ROY MERKIN

THIS IS A GENUINE RARE BIRD BOOK

Rare Bird Books
6044 North Figueroa Street
Los Angeles, CA 90042
rarebirdbooks.com



FIRST TRADE HARDCOVER EDITION



For more information, address:
Rare Bird Books Subsidiary Rights Department
6044 North Figueroa Street
Los Angeles, CA 90042

Set in Dante
Printed in the United States

10 9 8 7 6 5 4 3 2 1

Library of Congress Cataloging-in-Publication Data available upon request

# Foreword

Rarely does a case so grizzly, so grotesque, capture the complete, undivided interest of the twenty-four-hour news cycle and its disseminators. As a journalist, my modus operandi (to speak on theme for a moment) is to seek the truth, tell it to the American public, and finally, move on to the next day's news. There is, however, one case that has stuck with me long past my final reporting, one case that I have never been able to move beyond. It is known, in the eyes of the public, as *The Silver Scream*, and, if you're reading this book, you've undoubtedly heard of it. However, the real truth of what happened during that fall and winter of 2018 has never been published, until now.

In the months following the killings, I have spent countless hours poring over documents and journals, news clippings and television reports (some done by this very author himself). All of this time was spent searching for the necessary elements that *begin* to paint a picture that is as close to the truth as one can possibly dream of achieving. The following is an account that, I believe, will serve as the best record of the events that happened during those months of unspeakable bloodshed. In addition to the aforementioned documents, this work was also made possible by painstaking hours finding and interviewing those who were most closely involved.

This being said, however, it is worth noting that we may never know precisely what happened during that interval of time. If the dead could talk, what a tale they would weave. If the killer revealed what lurked behind their devilish eyes, we might begin to understand how the events unfolded. And if certain pieces of evidence had not been destroyed, they might have revealed a picture in far greater detail than we now find possible. In these absences, some liberties have been taken as to the mindset of the killer and the victims. These liberties are not taken lightly, but rather with the utmost care and meticulous extrapolation. Too often a journalist may be so excited to find an answer to a question that even an incorrect puzzle piece can be made to fit. I assure you, dear reader, that I have resisted the temptation to jump to any conclusions within this book and everything that you will read is factual, corroborated evidence, stitched together to form the most complete and accurate delineation possible.

One set of tools that we were fortunate enough to stumble upon are the notes of Doctor Ian Black. These notes take us not only into the mind of the doctor himself, but also of his most infamous patient, detailing their sessions in the process. Of particular importance are the notes regarding the patient's dreams, reprinted here in *italics* so as to convey an entree into the alternate reality of the subconscious. They are also expressed in present tense, as originally transcribed in the doctor's actual notes.

Also at our disposal, and certainly an instrument that is worth noting, is the knowledge that these killings emulated those depicted in various films of the horror canon. This discovery made it possible to insert some of the details from these films and, thereby, extrapolate on the events themselves; it is a coloring between the lines, where only gray existed. In closing, I remind you that all of this effort, from research to recording, has been made in an attempt to better understand, and make sense of, the horrific elements that make up:

*The Silver Scream.*

# I
# The American Nightmare

*How did that twat Colin Barlow make the cover of bloody Psychiatry Now?* The thought had consumed the usually brilliant mind of Doctor Ian Black ever since he had rifled through the mail earlier that Monday morning. *How had his former rival at Oxford been published before he was?* They had always managed to be neck and neck in the class rankings back home in his native England. Now, however, it appeared that after twenty years in the field, Barlow had struck a crippling blow.

In these morning hours, the doctor found himself reflecting on his life and very existence in his nondescript office on the outskirts of Salem, Massachusetts. Here he was, at forty-six years of age, practically unpublished compared to Colin Barlow's endless streak of pop-psychology ramblings; it burned him up inside. Years ago, he began writing a book on serial killers, his particular area of interest, but he never could hone the thesis enough to make it past the first few chapters. He knew that his own work was certainly more important than Colin's. Sure, he had always leaned away from the lightness of psychology and toward the darkest of cases—the darkest of minds—but, nevertheless, minds still worth exploring, perhaps even more so. Maybe if he hadn't given so much time to his patients, maybe if he'd spent more time researching, or perhaps if he was a bit more mainstream, he might have beaten Barlow to such an honor. However, Doctor Black had never grasped the notion of *publish or perish*, and now it seemed he was doomed to the latter (much like the victims of the serial killers that he had fixated on in his work).

Sometimes when he was most upset, his pain would manifest itself physically. A trait he rather disliked in himself but as a psychologist knew that he should forgive. It was certainly easier for him to give advice to a patient than to follow it himself. The pain, much like the sharp stab of a knife to the gut, almost always presented itself in the underside of his protruding belly, an area that had become even more pronounced as he approached his fifties. Like the slice of a blade, it would come on excruciatingly quickly, only to dissipate almost as expeditiously as it had arrived, offering him a breath of relief shortly thereafter. This time however, he could not have known that the feeling would lodge there for the months to come, as he would soon find himself teetering on the edge of purgatory, his life weighed in the balance. The pain had begun with Barlow, but it would move well beyond him—beyond even Doctor Black himself.

*Should he call Barlow to congratulate him? What? And give him the satisfaction!?* He couldn't possibly bear to have the metaphorical knife driven deeper. Besides, he had a big day ahead and a new patient with whom he was just beginning to work. The focus needed to shift off of publishing (or the lack thereof) and onto the patients, just as it always had for Doctor Black.

He needed to focus on a distraction. He looked around at his plain, beige room with its nondescript carpeting and bluish-gray couch. The unexciting couch and its equally sad coffee table served as the main focal point of an otherwise dull existence. On his wooden desk, clutter every which way, surrounding his laptop and phone system. In the corner of the office sat a TV on a stand showing a newscast. The news proved just the trick to distract him, as it offered a feature story by his favorite local newswoman, Lara Lambesis. Lara was gorgeous; she had a tight body, ethnically ambiguous olive skin, and ombre-colored hair that she wore long, its natural waves cascading below her shoulders and onto her chest. He always liked watching her and began to fantasize about what he might do if she were in front of him. He imagined her skin smelled of orchids and he would catch just a whiff of it as he softly kissed the flesh of her neck. It was difficult to concentrate on the newscast with the sexuality that exuded from Lara. Had the doctor been able to hone in on what she was saying, he might have heard the report of a string of teen suicides in the upstate New York town of Clifton Park. A whole town with a psychiatric problem and national news attention might have been just the thing to make his career. Instead, the doctor found himself staring at Lara's chest, imagining her in front of him wearing far less than the already-skimpy outfit she wore on television; imagining himself peeling it off to expose her soft, fleshy breasts that almost seemed too large for her petite body. And just as the thoughts of Colin seemed to drift away, and thoughts Lara took over, BZZZZ!! The noise emanated from his telephone system where a red light was simultaneously illuminated to accompany the blaring sound. At the other end, and just a room away, Karen, his new receptionist, gleefully shouted through the speaker, "Call for you, Doctor Black."

"And the caller is...?" replied Doctor Black, reminding her once again that she must always get a name if he is to be bothered by a phone call.

"It's someone named Colin Barlow?" she responded, finally getting the hang of her new-ish job.

Doctor Black sighed, "Put him through." It seemed as though Barlow had again beaten him to the punch, managing to do precisely the thing he had hoped to avoid; his day would now be further disrupted.

He feigned a smile and picked up the receiver. "Colin, you old so-and-so! What a wonderful article. I was just thumbing through it now," he said as he began to draw devil horns on Colin's face.

"Ah, yes, thrilling indeed, Ian, old boy. No hard feelings then?" Colin said on the other end of the line. Had the doctor's voice given him away? Was he not enthusiastic enough? He gripped his desk in defense of letting his jealousy show through.

"No, no...of course not!" replied the doctor, trying harder to feign enthusiasm while also drawing a Hitler mustache onto Colin's upper lip on the cover of the magazine. "I'm glad for you. It's a major accomplishment and it couldn't have happened to a better bloke!"

"Good...good. Well, I just thought I'd call to check in," said Colin, beginning to twist the knife. "I know there was some competitiveness between us back at school and I wanted...you know...to make sure we were...um, you know..." Colin was stumbling around for the words to cause Doctor Black to lash out; he was toying with him now. "No hard feelings between us. My getting published before—"

"No, certainly not. Certainly not!" Doctor Black interrupted. His nails dug deeper into the wood, scraping it as a zoo animal trying to escape its cage. "Rising tide raises all boats and what not. You've been focusing more on the research side, I've been focusing on helping my patients." He was spiraling now. Losing control as the pain to his stomach cut deeper. "Not a grumble in sight mate, but I've actually got a patient due any mo' so I'll have to let you go! Ta-ta! Until the next reunion!"

He hung up. *Was that as bad as it seemed to be?* How could he be so foolish as to let Colin get the best of him twice in one day? *Smarmy little git.*

There was some truth, however, in his need to get off the phone; his new patient was due any minute now. He had been waiting for the patient's files to transfer from his last therapist. Doctor Black's assistant was supposed to be in charge of these matters and it angered him that she had yet to deliver the files to his desk. "KAREN!" he bellowed, storming out of his office and toward the reception desk in the waiting room.

Karen Strode had become accustomed to such outbursts even after only a few weeks on the job. This one, however, in its suddenness and magnitude, caused her to spill the iced coffee she slowly sipped throughout the day, a routine that left her front teeth slightly stained between bleachings. Concern for her appearance did Karen well; she was twenty-four years old and drop-dead gorgeous. She knew it had been one of the reasons that she had gotten this job, but a paycheck is a paycheck, even if the doctor's leering occasionally creeped her out. In her life prior to the job, Karen had always made sure to dress well, even if it wasn't about getting ahead. Today was no exception, as she stunningly pulled off a black and red jumper, horizontally striped, tight-fitting to her breasts and flowing out at the midsection, giving her a youthful appearance. Her wavy brown hair, pulled tight to the sides, flowed free to the back, another style that made her appear younger than her already girlish appearance. Her pale skin was flawless, no doubt a result of her intense regimen, coupled with genetic fortune.

Karen quickly mopped up the iced coffee with some spare napkins as Doctor Black began his inquisition. "Karen? Have Spencer Charnas's patient transfer files arrived yet?"

"Not yet," she replied. "I've—"

"Did you call?" he interrupted, knowing full well the end of that sentence wouldn't have pleased him in the slightest.

"Uh...I emailed their office, but I haven't heard back," said Karen.

"EMAILED?!" He bellowed. "Karen, you've got a beautiful mouth, why don't you put it to use and get on the telephone!" The doctor settled himself before continuing, "I need to know why Doctor Michaelson's office requested that I take this patient and, apparently, this Charnas fellow's a burgeoning rockstar, first impressions, hmm?"

Finished with his tirade, Doctor Black returned to his office. As soon as he turned away, Karen rolled her eyes. It had only been a few days and already he could make her skin crawl, but she knew he was harmless overall. She'd always thought of him as a lonely old curmudgeon. Besides, even when he was belittling her or behaving wildly inappropriately for the workplace, his British accent seemed to let him off the hook. He always sounded so intelligent regardless of what came out of his mouth. At least in Karen's mind.

Re-entering his office, Doctor Black quickly rushed to turn off the television, throw away the magazine emblazoned with the likeness of that bastard Doctor Colin Barlow, and neaten his messy office in anticipation of his imminent appointment. Moments after beginning his task, in walked Karen. "Doctor Black?" she timidly said, continuing, "Mr. Charnas is here."

"Well now that he's here, what about his transfer files? Have they come through?" he clapped back.

Caught off guard, she slowly responded, "What?" remembering, "Oh, no…they didn't pick up…the phone. I did the phone this time, but I left a message—"

Doctor Black grumbled an unintelligible response, cutting her off. A silence overtook the room for a moment as she stood there, waiting for a next order. Surprised at her inability to understand the obvious next move, Doctor Black shooed her away, saying, "well… don't keep him waiting!"

Karen turned on a dime, flicking her hair around as she spun. She called into the waiting room for Spencer. Watching her go, Doctor Black muttered under his breath, "What am I even paying you for?" Karen heard him, but chose not to respond, thinking it better for all parties.

A moment later, Doctor Black's newest patient strode across the waiting room and toward the door to the office, his rockstar essence taking over the room like flames in a dry house, engulfing it all in an instant. As the charismatic front man of the band Ice Nine Kills, Spencer Charnas had always been used to fans gushing over him, but he never imagined that a psychologist like Doctor Black might do the same.

Upon meeting the high-profile patient, Doctor Black's nervousness leaked out in the form of a breathless gasp. An awkward moment went by before he spoke again. "Ahhhhh, Spencer," he finally gushed. "May I call you Spencer?" he asked, quickly catching his over-familiarity.

Attempting to reply, Spencer started, "Well sure—"

Immediately upon hearing this Doctor Black began, "Excellent, Spencer," getting more used to the name, "why don't you take a seat and we can get up to speed on your treatment thus far?"

Spencer moved into the office and toward the couch. His fitted leather jacket opened a bit as he walked, revealing a T-shirt with an upside-down cross emblazoned on the left breast. As he sat, the jacket creeped up his arms, revealing the bottom of a tattoo on his right forearm, the tail end of a full sleeve. He sat, his eyes level with those of Doctor Black, who noticed for the first time Spencer's perfectly coiffed, slicked back hair. *This was real rockstar material*, thought Doctor Black. And he was here for therapy, in his office. If the public only knew he was coming here, what it could do for his career.

"So, Spencer," Doctor Black began. "I'm afraid Doctor Michaelson's office failed to forward your session notes in time for today's session."

"And I doubt they ever will."

"Really? What makes you say that?"

"Well, just the suddenness of Doctor Michaelson's practice shutting down. You know, I'd been working with him for two years?"

Doctor Black lit up inside. *This could be a big payday, as well as some excellent press if he would be working with Spencer for this long… and, of course, the chance to help a potentially troubled individual,* he reminded himself.

"And out of the blue, he drops me," Spencer continued. "Without warning, over email no less! I've started thinking of him as 'Freudy Krueger.' I feel a bit betrayed really."

"Absoltively," replied Doctor Black. He had a peculiarity for managing to sound more British than the Queen herself when he became excited.

Spencer's face quickly turned to confusion at Doctor Black's seeming joy over the betrayal of a former doctor.

"I just mean…well, never mind," Doctor Black managed. "Fresh start then. New blood and all that, eh?" he said, changing the subject. "Now, down to business. I hope you don't mind if I record this session. It helps when I want to review something."

"Sure," replied Spencer as he watched the doctor hit a red button on a black digital recording device that sat on the coffee table. "I'm used to being recorded. Music career and all."

"Ha, ah yes, very good," laughed the doctor. "So, Spencer. Could you start by telling me what was going on in your life that made you seek therapy initially, or this time around?"

"Well, Doc, it's kinda…I feel like it sounds silly, but I've been having these really disturbing nightmares," Spencer replied sheepishly. "It's been hard to fall asleep, but then most nights, when I do, they wake me up..."

"From a deep sleep, would you say?" he interjected, attempting to clarify exactly what difficulties Spencer was facing.

"...Screaming. Sometimes. I was going to say," Spencer said, finishing his thought.

"Well, Spencer, it's good that you've taken the first step and come in. You shouldn't feel *silly* about feeling the way you feel, though. These feelings are a part of you, it'd be like being embarrassed of your eye color."

"Are you saying that no one is embarrassed by the color of their eyes?" Spencer shot back.

"To the contrary! If everyone were content with themselves I'd never keep the lights on, would I?" he joked. "What I'm saying is you need never feel embarrassed about yourself, least of all with me. Why don't we start with some of your dreams. Did you have one last night? Could you describe it to me? Do you remember these dreams, by the way?"

"Well, there was one recurring one, in particular," replied Spencer, as he began to recount the dream. "There's this girl..."

"Do you know this girl?"

"No, but she actually looks very similar to your receptionist, Karen. I'll call her Karen to keep it simple and give her a name. She's young. She's in high school. And I'm afraid for her."

"Why? What does she have to be afraid of?"

"It sounds crazy, but there's this entity. Almost, uh, I guess, I would call it a dream demon. And it haunts her nightmares," he offered, slowly.

"So the girl in your nightmares has nightmares herself?" asked the doctor, intrigued at the notion. "Very interesting."

"This entity can hurt her in her dreams, but in real life too. It's as if her dreams are spilling over into reality. Kids are dying in town, and they think it's suicide. But it's not. It's this entity killing them..."

*A girl who looks just like Karen is sitting in an auditorium of a high school listening to a speaker give a eulogy for a girl who has died. The stage is set with a podium and two easels. One of the easels features a poster for suicide prevention, while the other holds a portrait of an attractive blonde teenager with the words 'Remember Heather' written underneath. A mix of tears and open sobbing are on display throughout the audience. The school has come to mourn the latest of a string of teen suicides. Instead of tears, a look of disgust sits on Karen's face, coinciding with her angst-ridden outfit of a black T-shirt with an unbuttoned, plaid top layered over it and ripped skinny jeans.*

*As a young male teacher with a thin beard and mustard-yellow colored sports coat speaks to the school, Karen rises abruptly, startling the curly haired boy in the pink shirt sitting behind her. Other students look at her with a confused look, unable to focus on the memorial service. Karen runs out of the auditorium as the students continue to stare at her.*

*Now she's in the street, heading to her house, but something stops her dead in her tracks. An ambulance is parked outside of her neighbor Glen Lane's house, its red lights flash across the neighborhood, casting their glow in the relatively dull daylight of the late afternoon. Paramedics race to load a stretcher as the sirens blare and his parents scream. Karen had grown up right near the Lanes and been over to their house so many times. Now she watches as Glen's parents mourn another teen death, standing outside in their driveway and clutching each other in sorrow. She and Glen had grown apart over the years, but she still could not face another person close to her losing their life; she has to get away from this horror. Her pace quickens as she continues home, unable to process the most recent loss.*

*Karen turns onto Elm Street and toward her childhood home. She enters her house, runs up the stairs, and throws her book bag onto the unmade bed in the center of her room. Aside from the bed, there is a white dresser with a mirror and two white end tables that flank the bed. A door leading to a closet sits in the far corner from the door to the room, and another door off to the left and behind the dresser leads into an ensuite bathroom. The walls of the bedroom are adorned with posters of metal and punk bands from the nineties, as well as photographs of her and her friends at various concerts. She starts to look at the photos tucked into the corners of the mirror above the dresser when, all of a sudden, out of the corner of her eye, her figure transforms in the mirror and her skin crawls with fear. She looks directly into the mirror, but the only image is of herself staring back at her startled face. For a moment, she had thought she saw a figure with severely burnt flesh wearing a brimmed hat. She had not been sleeping well, so perhaps she could chalk it up to that.*

*One of the photographs in the mirror catches her eye as she turns away. It is of her and Heather, the girl from the poster at the memorial. Karen begins to rip up that photograph, then another, and another, not stopping until all of the photographs are ripped to shreds and sitting on her chest of drawers beneath the mirror. She grabs a lighter, ready to put flame to the photographs, but thinks better of it and pushes them off the chest and into the waste bin beside it.*

*Later that night, Karen is ready for bed. Another vain attempt at rest that she hopes will finally come after the last few sleepless nights. She pulls the covers up over the black T-shirt that she still wears and clicks out the light from the lamp on the nightstand.*

*For a while she is tossing and turning in her white and black floral sheets, unable to fall asleep. Finally, without noticing, as people do every night, in every corner of the world, she drifts off. As she sleeps, she continues to flail about, and is eventually awoken by the figure of a man standing beside her bed. He is a dream demon, of sorts, and stands six feet tall, in a brimmed fedora and the burnt flesh that she knew she had seen in the mirror hours before. He wears a red and black striped sweater and, when he holds one of his hands up to his lips, she notices that he has knives for fingers. Karen screams, she begins kicking and flailing her body, trying to get away, but to no avail. A large hand reaches up from within her bed and wraps its fingers around her, pulling her down. Instantly, she slips through the bed and falls, eventually landing on another bed, exactly the same as the one that she just left. She is back in her room. Alone, quiet, safe. The dream demon is gone.*

*Karen rises from the bed. She looks around, ready in case he should return. It seemed so real, but maybe it was only a nightmare. Out of an abundance of caution, she grabs a baseball bat from her closet. She picks up the bat and turns back toward the bed, immediately finding herself face to face with the dream demon who has returned once again. She clutches the bat, winds it up, and swings right through his face. Just as she is about to connect, he disappears, causing her to miss. He immediately reappears. She is dumbstruck. He slashes at her with the knives that replace his fingers, catching her across the stomach, gashing to top layers of her skin and drawing blood. Just as she reaches down to survey the damage, Karen wakes up. She is back in her bed. Safe again. It was only a nightmare. The dream demon is gone.*

*Awake in her bed, Karen feels the burning sensation of pain in her side, similar to that from the dream. She rises and stumbles into the bathroom connected to her bedroom. Clutching her side, she reaches the sink where she places her hands on either side of the white alabaster basin. Steadying herself through the excruciating pain, she lifts her head up to look into the double-wide mirror before pulling herself upright. She lifts her black T-shirt to reveal four gashes across her stomach, as if made by the knife-fingers of the dream demon. The red blood feels hot to the touch as she pokes at her wound. Karen comes to the realization that her dreams have crossed into the realm of reality.*

*Desperate to keep herself from sleeping again, and thereby dreaming again, Karen attempts to stay awake for as long as possible. She is sitting in a chair, watching television, trying to keep her mind alert. Eventually, sleep's weight hangs on her and her head limply nods forward.*

*Karen wakes up against the wall of her bedroom. The dream demon is across the room in front of her, his hand raised and threateningly twisted into a choking position. From a nine-foot distance, she feels his hand grasp her neck, suffocating her as he closes his finger-knives together from across the room. He grits his teeth and manipulates the burnt lips of his horribly disfigured face into a smile. As the dream demon lifts his hand, Karen feels herself rising from the floor and toward the ceiling, held only by this mysterious force that wraps itself around her neck. Suddenly, he thrusts his hand backward and she flies onto the bed. The jolt of the movement awakens her. She is suddenly back in front of the television. Awake in the real world.*

*Karen continues to mindlessly watch the TV screen, trying to stay awake. Suddenly she watches it flicker until it reveals the dream demon who is smiling back at her through her television set. He quickly disappears, leaving her to wonder if she is awake or dreaming. Is there a difference?*

*Eventually, Karen's head nods forward, sleep again wins over, and she is mysteriously back in her bed. This time, however, her bed is surrounded by a street. It is her street, lined by trees with grass and sidewalks surrounding them, but this version of her street is darker and more deserted than she has ever experienced.*

*Karen walks back toward her house, seeking the theoretical safety that might await her. From the corner of Elm and Orange Grove, she walks past a lamppost. As she continues, she feels something—or someone—over her shoulder. Slowly, she turns around. There before her sleepy eyes is the dream demon, leaning on the post. He smiles and waves, teasing her before he strikes. She sprints away as fast as her legs will carry her; she is running to survive. As she runs, she does not come to her house, instead she finds herself back at the very corner that she was running away from. She is once again face to face with the dream demon. She runs away again, only to find herself back in the starting position for yet a third time. Once more she tries to run, and once again, the same result. She is broken. There is no exit. She succumbs to the dream demon, kneeling down in defeat. She looks up to meet the gaze of her soon-to-be killer. He smiles, grabs her chin with his left hand, and winds up his right hand ready to slash his "fingers" across her neck. She uses her right hand to grab onto his black and red striped sweater, clutching it in her tightened fist as she braces herself. Just as the moment of impact arrives, she disappears. His attempt to strike her is foiled and the dream demon finds only the air as he spins around from the momentum.*

*Karen wakes up on the floor of her living room in front of the television. Around her, a broken chair, two of its wooden legs cracked in half. She survived, she is awake. The chair and its real-world fall has woken her up, saving her from surefire death. Karen feels that she is clenching something in her right fist. She looks down and sees that she has a piece of the sweater from the dream demon. A thought immediately crosses her mind as she ponders the idea that if she could take a piece of his sweater, perhaps she could bring the whole demon into the real world, where he might be vulnerable to her attacks; just as he can hurt her in his world, she could hurt him in the real world.*

*Karen prepares a device that can be set to a timer to deliver herself an electric shock at a certain point, thereby waking her body up. She splices together the ends of her alarm clock with an electrical charge, completing the circuit through her stomach. She connects two conductive pads to the ends of the wires and sticks them onto her stomach, right over her previous wound, thereby creating the greatest chance for pain, and a higher chance that she will wake up. She picks up her baseball bat, lays down on the bed, and attempts to fall asleep. She is ready. She would once again return to this other world, ready for a fight, and ready to bring that fight back to her turf.*

Spencer went silent for a moment. Having recounted the dream to the best of his ability. The doctor, however, was hooked, ready to hear more. "And? Then what happened?" he eagerly asked.

"Oh…I don't know. I just wake up. But what the hell are dreams anyway? Huh, Doc?"

The doctor thought for a moment, before continuing, "Yes, well, I can see why this would all be…very troubling. Was there anything else that's been troubling you? In your life, I mean. Not that these dreams aren't enough, I just mean—is there anything else you would like to discuss?"

"No, it's a pretty great life, I gotta say. If there's one thing, it's sometimes the guys in the band."

"How so?" replied the doctor.

"Sometimes they just give me a hard time on tour. Like if I disappear for a little while to go do an interview or I show up late for a sound check. But, it's tough getting to everything. I just have more commitments than they do." As he spoke, Spencer began to play with a Rubik's Cube that he found on the desk. "I tell them all the time that they can go out and make their own brands and opportunities. You know. Or, find their own promotional events with companies. They just don't do it."

"Yes, yes. I can see that might be difficult," acknowledged the doctor. "But, if I may. I do have one more question about this dream."

"Sure."

"Out of curiosity, where were *you* while it was all happening? With the girl and the demon entity. Where were you *perceiving* it from?"

Spencer continued to twist the sides of the Rubik's Cube, turning them quickly until one of the faces was completely red. He then looked up and answered the question. "I wasn't anywhere in particular, I guess. I was just sort of everywhere, watching it unfold."

"Ah," the doctor continued. "Well, unfortunately, when it comes to matters of the mind, there are no shortcuts, no...silver bullets. If we are going to get to the bottom of these dreams, and what's causing them, it could take weeks of rigorous therapy, maybe even months."

"I figured that, Doctor, and I'm willing to put in the work." Spencer replied, now moving onto the orange face of the Rubik's Cube.

"Excellent, excellent," the doctor began to mutter to himself. "Maybe even years," he added, mumbled under his breath where he thought Spencer couldn't hear it. He was becoming giddy with excitement inside at the prospect that this patient might stay with him for such a long span of time, greatly increasing his chances for both fame and fortune.

"Years!?" asked Spencer upon hearing his doctor's mumbled suggestion.

"What? Oh, no, no. I was, uh, thinking of something else," the doctor quickly shot back. The doctor nervously chuckled to himself. He laughed a lot when he was nervous, a trait he worried sometimes gave too much away. Collecting himself, he continued, "I think in the meantime, some kind of sleeping aid should be in order—and helpful—fortunately, my colleague across the hall is a psychiatrist, and she might be able to write you up a quick script for something. Just to help you get through the night, so to speak. I'll just pop over the hall and ask her and be back in a mo', okay?"

Spencer nodded, "Sounds good. Especially if you think it would help..."

Doctor Black exited his office and dashed across the hallway to the office of Doctor Nancy Price, the license psychiatrist with whom he shared a common waiting room, and their receptionist, Karen. As he passed through, Karen looked up from her phone, attempting to stop him with her hand, adding, "She's having lunch, she asked that she not be disturbed." Ignoring her, Doctor Black flung open the door to his colleague's office, knocking as he was halfway into the room.

Doctor Price kept a neat office, much neater than that of her colleague. Bookshelves lined the interior walls and a large fern sat in each corner, aside from that with the door. On the opposite side, the windowed walls of a corner office let light pour through, illuminating her couch and end tables that held possessions, acquired on her travels. An avid adventurer, Nancy Price had been to many parts of the world, usually on humanitarian missions, collecting items as she went. Behind her large oak desk, two reddish paintings gave a warm, yet tribal, feel to the room. Unlike that of her colleague, this room had life and energy, a vibrancy that coincided with that of its occupant. Doctor Price herself was in her late twenties, sexy and smart-looking at the same time. While it made it hard for people to take her seriously at first, they quickly learned that she was a genius hidden inside a model's frame. Her brown hair with its highlights always looked best just as it was arranged today, half up with the sides pulled back into a bun, and the rest falling just above the small of her back.

As Doctor Black entered, he found his colleague at her desk eating lunch while simultaneously looking over a stack of notes in a manilla file. She held a plastic fork in her hand as she mindlessly munched her Caesar salad with grilled chicken, having not taken her eyes off of the file for the moments before he entered. The noise of the doctor coming in caused her to jerk her head up and quickly display an expression of annoyance at the intrusion. "Ian! What do you want? I have a patient in fifteen," she barked.

"Not to worry, it will only take a moment," he said, shutting the door behind him. "I have a patient that I need to send in. It should be just a quick script and then on with your lunch. He just needs something to help his sleep. Been having some nightmares, is all."

She sighed, knowing that part of their deal for the office space made her prescription pad available to Doctor Black's patients, as well as her own. "Send him in," she said in defeat. "Who is this person?"

"Spencer, the musician bloke I was telling you about."

"Oh. Right. Okay, let me just straighten up a bit here." she said, throwing her salad to the side and putting her file away. "You can send him in whenever."

Doctor Black turned on his heels, opening the door to Doctor Price's office and leaving it open as he went back toward his own office. He ushered Spencer out, escorting him into the office across the hall and leaving him in the capable hands of Doctor Price before returning to make some notes and debrief before his next patient would arrive.

Within ten minutes, Spencer had recounted the details of some of his dreams for Doctor Price. She sat in disbelief, shocked that a person could get any sleep with such vivid, gruesome nightmares haunting him. As soon as he finished, she reassured him that this was the right thing to do, saying "with dreams like that, no wonder you can't get any sleep. I'm going to give you something to help."

"Thanks, Doctor Price. I really appreciate it," replied Spencer.

"Oh, you can call me Nancy," she added. "Doctor Black prefers to be called doctor, but I find that a bit pretentious." As she spoke, she removed a set of small keys from her wrist and inserted one into the top drawer of her desk, from which she removed a thick prescription pad.

"Thank you, Nancy," said Spencer, trying out the name. A portrait behind her caught his eye, and he pointed to it. "Is that a picture of an elephant over there? Who is that riding it?"

Nancy turned, looking at the photo behind her and leaving her pad on the desk. "That's me, actually," she said with the unexcited tone of someone embarrassed by all that they have seen and done.

"That's you?!" responded Spencer, prodding for more detail. "May I see it?" He stood up, hoping to get a closer look.

"Sure," she said, standing up as she responded. She turned around to pick up the framed image.

"Where was that taken, Doctor? Sorry. Nancy," Spencer corrected himself as he leaned over the desk toward Nancy's back. She was unaware of his movements.

"Africa," she replied, picking up the photograph. Her back turned to Spencer, she looked at the picture, reminiscing of the amazing, once-in-a-lifetime trip. "After I completed my residency, some friends and I volunteered for Doctors Without Borders. And it was probably the greatest experience of my life." While she spoke, Spencer had moved his hand across the desk, palmed her prescription pad, and started sliding it toward his pocket.

"Is that where you got that figure, too?" he asked, her back still turned.

Nancy abruptly turned around at the question. As she did so, Spencer slid his hand into the pocket of his coat, concealing the prescription pad as he did so. "What?!" she spat. Spencer pulled his hand out of his pocket to point to a statue of a woman located to the right of the photograph. "Oh," she laughed, understanding what he was referring to. "No, while that is technically a fertility icon, it's actually just a reproduction. I think it's from Home Restorations."

Nancy sat back down and Spencer followed suit. She spent a moment collecting herself and looking around. She could have sworn that she had placed a pad of prescription sheets on her desk, but yet, they were not there. She shrugged it off as absent-mindedness and pulled out another set from her top drawer and began to write the prescription.

As Nancy wrote, Spencer asked her, "Tell me, when was the last time someone told you that you were a fascinating woman?"

Nancy laughed coquettishly, as she continued to write. She was flattered, but this was a professional relationship.

"This is for five miligrams of diazepam." she deflected. "But it's not a permanent solution."

"Trust me, your signature will give me more relief than you know, Nancy," Spencer replied, quizzically. "Thank you." His hand lingered over hers as he received his script. He took the prescription, folded it, and put it into the back pocket of his black jeans before exiting her office. Nancy stared at the door, watching him go. Spencer had caused a feeling of unease in her that she could not immediately quantify. He reminded her of someone from her past. She was attracted to him. Ever since high school, she had always had a thing for musicians; it never ended well, particularly that first love. After a moment of reflection and reminiscence, she returned to her salad. Hopefully her next patient would be a few minutes late, giving her time to eat.

Doctor Black sat in his office with the television on, tuned to the local news station where Lara Lambesis was once again reporting on a mysterious string of teen suicides in upstate New York. As he started to listen, he realized that it bore a resemblance to what Spencer had just recounted. The thought was quickly interrupted by a knock on his door. Spencer poked his head in to thank the doctor and note that he would see him in a couple of weeks following his next string of show dates. After a brief exchange of pleasantries he left and the doctor once again turned his attention to the television, but he had missed the story. He thought to research it further but was immediately distracted by the *Psychiatry Now* magazine in his wire mesh wastebasket, Colin Barlow's idiotic smile peeking out from the side.

# II
## Thank God It's Friday

It was the second Friday after he had first met Spencer and Doctor Black's head snapped back against his overly large deep blue office chair out of boredom and anticipation while he let out a deep sigh. He spun his chair a few times, idly fidgeting as he waited impatiently for the newest patient to arrive for his second appointment. Five minutes turned to ten, which turned to Spencer finally arriving, Karen yelling instead of using the intercom, and the doctor sitting immediately upright in his chair, ready to greet his rockstar patient. Spencer strode in, apologized for his tardiness (something about an early hockey game at a nearby arena causing traffic), and plopped down on the grayish-blue couch.

"Well, Spencer," began Doctor Black, holding back his annoyance, "You're here now, and that's what matters. How was… Texas, was it?"

"Texas, yeah. Great. Some of our best fans are down there, so it was a lot of fun. Stopped at the Alamo when we played San Antonio. Looked at Cadillac Ranch."

"Excellent, excellent. Could I get you some water?"

"No thanks, Doc, I brought my own," Spencer said, holding up the bottle he almost always seemed to have with him, causing Doctor Black to relax back into his chair, now wheeled over toward Spencer.

"How are things with the band, overall? Last time you spoke about some trouble between a few of you?"

"Ah, that. Yeah, they still give me a hard time for disappearing here and there, but it's no big deal. I'm not really doing anything important, sometimes I just need a minute away."

"I thought you said it was business that was calling you away," said the doctor.

"Oh, yeah. Business too, sometimes. With this industry, it's like you're constantly swimming upstream, you know? You just need a break to catch a breath of fresh air once in a while."

"I understand," replied the doctor, writing down some notes as he did. "And how are things going with the dreams? Are you still having them?"

"Dreams? Yep, still having them..." answered Spencer, slowly. As he did, he stroked his hair back across his head.

"Even with the...Diazepam?" the doctor questioned, gesturing to Nancy's office as he did, indicating that he knew what she had prescribed him. The doctor also knew that, while it may not have solved the issue, it had hopefully brought his most prominent patient some relief, and that patient would, in turn, tell others. He did not at all care for the fact that his career rested so heavily on the pharmacology expertise of Doctor Nancy Price, but such is life in the game of minds.

"Yeah, it kept the dreams down for a week or so. Then on the tour they started coming back. Maybe worse even."

"Is it the same imagery we discussed before? With the girl?" queried the doctor, his interest piquing, as he found himself further drawn into Spencer's affliction.

"No, well, she's there too, and another girl, kinda like your attractive colleague actually, Dr. Nancy. But I'm also there now, not just a spectator. Oh, and also all the guys from my band. They're there too."

"I see, that's an interesting change. And what are you doing?" He took a sip of his own water without glancing away from Spencer. He was hanging on to every word of this fascinating case.

"There was this recurring dream that I had. It spanned a couple of nights. I can try to describe it for you if you want."

The doctor nodded. "Sure, go ahead."

Spencer began to unfold the dream for the rapt therapist: "It's the last night of overnight summer camp and I'm a counselor....

*Spencer is sitting around a glowing campfire that ineffectively flickers its light on the deep green forest that completely surrounds the open area of the fire with its endless void of darkness. A group of counselors are tightly sat around the campfire in the middle of the woods. Some of the counselors are the members of Spencer's band, JC, Patrick, and Julio, but also present are Doctor Nancy Price and the receptionist, Karen. Most wear white T-shirts with the words "Crystal Lake Camp" splashed across them. They sing a song, unaware that a row of deceased ghost counselors wearing the same T-shirts sing along in unison behind them. The song continues as other counselors pack up the camp for the summer, closing up the boat house, stacking oars. As the living counselors begin to peel off, the ghosts continue singing, using their song as a warning to the living to leave while they still can.*

*Preparations for an end of summer party begin. Julio goes to get a funnel and some sort of neon green liquid; he's planning on winterizing the pipes, readying them for the off-season before attending the party. As the counselors pour into a large wooden building labeled "Staff Cabin," they bring a wave of beers, snacks, and a guitar. Having decided that the camp is ready enough, they begin to ready themselves for getting wasted.*

*In a large bathroom with rows of showers, Julio stands at a urinal. He is about to funnel the green liquid through the pipes but thinks to use the urinal first. With a cigarette hanging from his mouth and a liquid-*

*filled funnel in his right hand, he uses the urinal. He casually minds his business unaware of what lurks behind him and across the bathroom. Suddenly, as if he came out of the pipes, a man in a hockey mask appears at the far end of the showers. He stealthily approaches Julio, who turns around, falling over his half-down pants and spilling the funnel, which creates a river of green that flows toward a drain in the middle of the floor. As he looks up, he sees there is no one behind him. He laughs it off, turns to resume peeing, pants still down, but is instead struck in the face by a large machete. Julio is killed instantly, his blood draining toward the center of the floor, lacing the green river with a deep scarlet. His body lies motionless in white, fluorescent light blaring from the ceiling. A voice screams out from the drain.*

Doctor Black interrupted Spencer's dream to clarify. "This voice that's calling out to you and the others here. Is it one of these ghost counselors?" he asked.

"More of a...motherly kind of figure. It's nurturing," Spencer corrected him, before continuing with his recount of the dream.

*Meanwhile, in the staff cabin, the counselors are singing, dancing, and partying, unaware of any trouble on the horizon. Patrick, now dressed in a loose black T-shirt dances with the girl who looks just Karen, the receptionist, now wearing a blue and white checkered crop top. They begin dancing closer to one another, as the other members of the band look on with a knowing acknowledgement. As if following the expectations of everyone in the room, they eventually sneak off together to the sleeping area of the large staff cabin. There they may find themselves some respite from the noise of the other counselors who drink and revel loudly at summer's end. JC checks his watch and then questions the others as to where Julio might have gotten to. They assume he's probably just jerking off somewhere and think nothing of it.*

*Each of the sleeping quarters in the staff cabin holds eight bunk beds, arranged along each of the four walls. Patrick and Karen have found themselves down the main hallway and inside the last room on the left. They are now making out in the bunk that typically belongs to JC, immediately to the left of the door and on the bottom. The room is pitch black with just a stream of light from the full moon creeping through the window beside the bunk. Karen sits astride Patrick, who has made quick work of removing her crop top, leaving only a pink swimsuit that she still had on underneath following the afternoon's activities. Their hot and heavy kissing prevents each of them from realizing that a red liquid now drips down Karen's back and onto Patrick's face below. Feeling something wet, Patrick opens his eyes, pausing mid-kiss for a moment to wipe away what he assumes to be the inevitable sweat from the late-summer Texas heat and is astonished to find a sticky, ruby-colored substance coming off of Karen. He wipes his face, further smearing the substance over himself. Wondering why he has stopped caressing her, Karen opens her eyes to find his face covered in blood. She screams, but most of the counselors aren't paying enough attention and few can hear her over the loud partying from the main room. The few counselors that think they might hear something dismiss it, chalking it up to Patrick's particular expertise.*

*After Karen screams, Patrick springs into action. He quickly notes that the blood is coming from the top bunk and leaps out of the bed to further explore. As he peeks his head over the side of the mattress, there to greet him is the body of his fellow counselor, Julio, stabbed through the face, a mess of blood and skin dripping off him like the rain off the cabin roof in a summer storm. Patrick recoils in horror, but there is little time to think, as he and Karen are confronted with a noise coming from the closet to their right. They jerk their heads around to investigate, landing their eyes on the closet with just enough time to see the large hockey-masked figure rushing toward him. Unable to escape, Patrick freezes up. The figure lifts his machete before slicing it across Patrick's awaiting neck, which sputters a few spurts of red blood before gushing the entire contents of his carotid artery onto the floor. Karen screams. She runs from the room, sprinting through the hall before plunging herself through the outside door and into the awaiting night.*

*The camp counselor who looks exactly like Doctor Nancy Price hears the screams from the other room and assumes them to be something other than teenage fun. She decides to investigate. Grabbing a couple of the others, she starts toward the sleeping area with Spencer and JC following closely behind. The three are stunned to find their coworkers' bodies lying lifeless within the chamber. Noting that Karen is missing, Nancy decides to head out after her. She grabs a lantern and beckons Spencer to go with her. He obliges and they both journey to see what lurks in the darkness.*

*JC races into the office, seeking out the main phone to call for help. He finds that the phone is dead and the line has been cut. He quickly realizes that he must act fast to save himself, as waiting for any help to arrive might take too long. Noticing a set of keys on the desk, JC grabs them and leaves the cabin, running toward the staff van, hoping he can use it to outpace whatever menace is loose in the camp.*

*Meanwhile, deep in the woods, Karen runs, each of her footstrokes cracking the underbrush, now browning with late-Summer. While the woods around her slowly begin their seasonal death, she is determined not to succumb to the same fate. She picks up the pace, moving as fast as her legs will carry her, before striking an errant stick emerging from the ground. It snaps and emits a loud crack that reverberates through the woods, as well as her body, and sends her tumbling head over heels and onto the ground. While pain rushes to her ankle, which rapidly swells, hope drains from her body. She realizes that she may never leave these woods alive. As she tries to get up, she hears another crack. This time not close by and not directly in front of her, but, instead, it comes from beyond the veil of trees that immediately surround her. Her eyes shoot up to reveal nothing but an endless sea of trees with barely any moonlight seeping through for visibility. She is lost, alone, injured, and in the dark. Hoping to find her way away from the camp and toward some safety, she gets up and begins to hobble in the direction that she had been heading. Focusing her eyes on her injured ankle, she loses sight of where she is going and suddenly bumps into a large tree that has somehow ended up in the middle of the path. Slowly, she looks up the massive trunk toward the top, where just two feet up from her face she sees a hockey mask staring back down at her. A machete is the next image that flashes in front of her eyes, quickly striking her neck, before penetrating downward in a stabbing motion that punctures through her left trapezius muscle and continues into her ribs. The masked man lifts the blade off of her body as she slides to the ground.*

*Meanwhile, JC arrives at the beat up old Econoline van before fumbling with the ancient key that must be inserted into the driver's side door to unlock it. His hand shakes as he misses the hole again and again, scratching the already-damaged paint job around the slot. Finally he hits his mark, flings open the door, and enters the van. He's nearly home free. He settles down and the keys glide effortlessly into the ignition. He bounces once on the seat to adjust his positioning and turns the key to start the van. The engine revs once before failing to turn over. He checks the shifter, making sure it is in park before giving it another go. Again, the van fails to start. One final time, the engine revs, it fires up. He puts it into drive and just as he thinks he's made it out alive, the engine dies before he can fully relish the thought. He turns the key back to the off-position and leaves it in the ignition. He gets out of the van and walks around the front to check under the hood.*

*Spencer and Nancy stalk the woods, Spencer armed with a tennis racket and Nancy with an axe, looking for whatever sadistic evildoer killed their friends. Spencer holds a lantern, which casts its light a few yards around them, but does little to illuminate the thick woods they have reluctantly entered. Moments uneventfully pass before they hear a cry of frustration coming from the direction they left. It's unmistakably JC's voice.*

*JC has opened the hood of the van and looks at an engine that is well beyond repair. Numerous rubber lines and wires have been slashed and fluid leaks from all corners of the vehicle. A hopeless task. He screams in frustration, echoing beyond the campgrounds and into the woods.*

*Assuming the worst, Nancy grabs Spencer's arm at the sound of JC's cry. She thrusts her body closer to Spencer in search of safety from whatever monster has attacked their co-counselors. As she continues down the path with Spencer, Nancy notices a familiar blue and white checkered fabric on the ground in the direction that they are heading. She pulls Spencer toward the discovery and, as they approach, they recognize Karen, lying dead, blood pooled around her neck and head. Spencer suggests that they head back to the main campground, that whatever is after them cannot be beaten through running but must be faced head on. Nancy nods in assent and they march back toward the camp, still armed with the racket and hatchet, braced for a fight.*

*JC finishes surveying the damage and turns back toward the woods, contemplating whether or not he should make a run for it. Within that instant of hesitation, he is struck in the chest by a flying hatchet that swirls out from the wooded void. The decision on whether or not to run has been made and he who has made the decision calmly emerges from the trees to collect his weapon. He surveys JC, who he finds to be still standing and attempting to scream but finding it impossible to do so through all of the fresh blood gurgling from his mouth. The masked killer penetrates JC straight through his neck with his machete, just for good measure. The man finishes by extracting both his machete and hatchet, using his boot to shove the lifeless body from both.*

*Nancy heads toward the camp, axe in hand, Spencer following behind. She is stopped dead in her tracks by a sound from the bushes. Spencer's brisk pace, coupled with this abrupt stop, causes him to trip over himself and bump into her back, further startling her. Nancy drops the lantern plunging them into darkness. She lets out a small screech that seems to hang in the air, echoing as it spreads out into the woods. They stare at each other through almost-complete darkness, immediately realizing the full weight of drawing any kind of attention to their location. Fearing that the masked man has been alerted to their presence, they begin a slow creep back to the camp. Before they can take even a few steps, they hear footsteps in the distance. The masked man thunders up a side path off of the main one and heads right toward them. At first they only hear his approach, but after a few more steps, they make out a shadowy figure against the moonlight. Nancy braces, clutching her axe. The masked man charges, ready to take on the last survivors. Nancy raises her weapon, determined that she will not go down without a fight. Her axe is raised as the masked man is within striking distance, she shuts her eyes and lowers the blade toward his direction, where it comes to a complete stop. The man catches the axe and wrestles it away from her, throwing her to the ground. He lifts his machete, ready to thrust it through her, when Spencer intercepts his attack with the tennis racket, catching the blade in the strings. Realizing they have limited time to run, Spencer shouts to Nancy to go with him. She gets up and starts running down the path after Spencer who has retained the machete caught in his racket.*

*Spencer and Nancy arrive at the waterfront where they load themselves into a stray red canoe that lingers by the shore, hoping that the monster's strength ends with the land. The canoe plunges into the smooth glass-like surface of the calm water sending out ripples as the two thrust themselves away from the camp in a panic. As soon as they are twenty feet off the land, the masked man again appears. He is stopped short in his tracks as the water starts. Seemingly afraid, he does not pursue the couple into the lake. Spencer and Nancy maintain their guard as they gently fall into a sleep, having escaped the camp.*

"Well, that's wonderful, isn't it? Real improvement there," Doctor Black chimed in. "Your dream protagonists survived. You survived."

"Not quite," Spencer corrected him. "I haven't finished my story just yet."

*The sun is just beginning to peek over the trees and onto the lake that supports a canoe holding a sleeping Nancy and Spencer. Spencer's arms are draped over Nancy, who rests between his legs, her head on his chest. In her right arm she holds the machete, the only fading artifact of the night of madness they have survived. Slowly, they wake up, revived by the sun's rays dancing across their faces. The canoe floats gently on the river as each breathes a sigh of relief, relishing in their escape.*

*This peace lasts only a fleeting moment, as, suddenly, the masked figure breaks the surface of the water right next to the canoe, flying like a cannonball toward the sky. He grabs for the machete, attempting to wrestle it from Nancy's arms, only to tip the canoe, plunging all three into the water. The canoe floats alone on the surface for a moment. Then another. The stillness returns to the lake as none of the three emerge.*

"...and *then* I wake up," finished Spencer.

"Not exactly the sort of soothing dreams one looks for when seeking uninterrupted sleep, is it? I can certainly see that," added the Doctor.

Spencer paused for a moment, seemingly for dramatic effect, as he had already thought of his next move. He knew that the drugs had worked a bit and attempted to seek out some more relief. "Can Doctor Price up my dosage of the Diazepam, you know, just to get me through this tour?" he queried. "I haven't had a full night's sleep in a week."

The doctor took a moment to consider and entertain this request. He knew that a prescription might be an easier course, and would certainly appease his client, yet he wanted to make sure he could gain as much information from Spencer, and as much credit for treating him, as possible before turning him over to the prescription pad of Doctor Price. After quickly weighing his options, he began, "Well, Spencer, as much as that might seem like an easy solution, I really think that getting to the core of what's causing the anxiety in the first place is the better plan." Spencer sighed, his attempt foiled. The doctor then added, "These drugs can become very addictive and they don't actually fix what's really wrong. Did the dreams start two years ago when you initially sought out Doctor Michaelson? Were there changes happening in your life then, perhaps?"

"No, actually, I've been having these nightmares going back a lot farther than that," Spencer replied.

"How far are we talking about here?"

"Probably from when I was a little kid."

"Interesting, and does anything from your childhood stand out as being the source of anxiety?" The doctor realized for the first time that he knew so little about Spencer's childhood. He made a note on his pad to research this on his own but thought that some more prodding might yield fruit as well, perhaps.

"Not really, I had a pretty normal life growing up," Spencer replied, dodging the question a bit. "How are we doing on time? I feel like the hour mark's coming up pretty quick," he added, further dodging any discussion of his earlier years.

"Well, sure it is," said the doctor, noticing the time. "But, I've got a few—"

"Oh no, that's fine, I don't want to go over my time. Wouldn't be fair," interrupted Spencer. "Next week we're in Detroit so... week after then, I guess? All righty?" Spencer grabbed his water bottle and started to leave. "See you in two weeks."

The doctor was caught off guard but still managed to call after Spencer, who was then halfway to the door, "Fair enough, let Karen know on your way out, and then we can really get to the bottom of things! All right?" he added, trying to gauge if Spencer was still within hearing distance. The abruptness of the exit puzzled him as he stared contemplatively at the door, engrossed in the enigma of his new patient.

# III
## Stabbing in the Dark

Doctor Black sat anxiously in his oversized chair, tapping his fingers on the black blotter pad on top of his desk in rhythmic synchronicity with the ticking clock on his office wall. In a few minutes his session with Spencer was meant to begin and he had just scribbled out a few notes leading up to the session. As an indication that the ever-shortening days of early fall had arrived, an orange light crept across his desk and onto his workspace. As he wrote these new notes, he remembered jotting down some old ones from his last session with Spencer. He had meant to review them in the interim but had failed to do so. Had he looked at them, he might have seen where he mentioned that he should have a look into Spencer's past prior to today's session. Instead, he flipped back to the page from that session now, giving him only a brief moment to reflect on his failing memory and not the actual content of his assignment before Spencer arrived.

Spencer entered ready to get down to business. He tucked his sunglasses into his leather jacket, which he promptly removed and laid neatly on the sofa, patting it down with his hand. "Can't believe I made it," he sighed. "Here on time for once, huh?"

"Nonsense, I hadn't noticed any previous tardiness." The doctor replied, lying to appease his patient. "Wonderful to see you, Spencer."

The doctor scooted his office chair over to the other side of the coffee table from Spencer's place on the couch. For a session such as this, he knew that having the closer intimacy of a face-to-face meeting might breed an easier discussion of Spencer's past. The doctor quickly cut any air of tension in the room with an attempt at a joke, "No time like the present to talk about the past, eh?"

Spencer chuckled slightly, unamused at the joke but unwilling to hurt his doctor's feelings. He then clapped his palms together, rubbing them quickly, and told the doctor, "I'm all yours. Let's get to it."

"So, in our last session, you seemed…reticent to delve into the memories of your childhood. I just feel like, if we can probe those childhood memories, it may help us get to the root cause of the problem," Doctor Black began. "As opposed to just regurgitating the same old new nightmares."

"It's funny that you say that," Spencer responded. "Because my most recent nightmares have been about myself as a child."

Knowing that dreams can be conflated with memories, particularly those from childhood, the doctor paused for a moment to consider his next question, mentally questioning if it were even answerable. "And you're sure it was a dream? And not a memory?"

"That's what was so strange about it," Spencer began slowly. "I'm dreaming about myself as a child, but also as a spectator. Sort of watching the story unfold from the outside." Spencer appeared to question his thoughts as he spoke, unsure of how to describe exactly what he had experienced.

"Well, that can be common in childhood recollections. If we're told something happened to us, but we can't quite remember it, we almost re-remember it, but in the third person. What happens in this particular—dream—for lack of a better word?"

"So, I'm a little boy, and I've got a babysitter, and she looks very much like your colleague, Doctor Price, er, Nancy." The doctor sat up a bit, discomforted by the familiarity that Doctor Price established with her patients. Spencer continued, "My parents are out of town, and she invites her friends over. And they bring booze and drugs and they invite guys over. But the guys that come over, are the guys from my band. And one of them has a girlfriend that looks just like your receptionist, Karen"

"So the members of this office? They're in the dream again?" Doctor Black interjected.

"It's hard to say," replied Spencer. "They look like them, yes."

"Sorry, just a point of clarification. So, you were saying?"

"I just remember being so nervous that my parents are going to come home and everyone's going to get into trouble."

"Trouble with your parents though, it's not exactly the grizzly stuff your nightmares are normally made of, now is it?"

"If only it were trouble with just parents," Spencer added. "I didn't tell you about the shadow man…"

*A clock ticks its approach to midnight. An imprisoned patient in a white uniform and shoes sits cross-legged on the floor of a white padded cell, the colorless monotony broken only by the glint of the patient's handcuffs and their matching steel bars that line the front of the cell. The clock strikes its hour and, seemingly on cue, a middle-aged guard, weary from his graveyard shift, enters the hallway of the ward for his nightly checks. His name badge indicates that his name is "Carlos." He uses his freedom to taunt the imprisoned man. First, he twirls his keys around his fingers, then he uses his fists to bang on the steel exoskeleton of the prisoner's cage. Unable to get a rise out of the unflappable resident, Carlos enters the cell, violating protocol. He taps the patient, yells at him, ultimately failing to stir him. Finally, he resorts to kicking the confined man. Nothing.*

*Suddenly, the patient reaches his hands up and in one motion wraps his fingers around Carlos' neck, lingering there for a brief moment. Slowly he strangles out all signs of life before continuing up toward the guard's eyes. The patient's nails penetrate the ocular region, quickly releasing the balls from their orbital socket with nothing more than a short pop and sustained squishing noise. The naked retinas gush blood, discoloring the white-washed scene with its crimson flow. A call comes over Carlos' radio, but death has rendered him deaf to its sound. Slowly, a manually controlled security camera turns its lens to the scene and shortly thereafter, an alarm blares and, in perfect syncopation, lights flash across the ward with their intermittent orange glow.*

*Elsewhere, an almost empty house is poised to fill up with teens ready to party. A young boy in a plain white T-shirt stares out a first-floor window of the open-planned living room area as his babysitter, who looks just like Doctor Nancy Price, is in the kitchen cutting limes with a knife far too large for the task. She wears tight jean shorts and a pink bikini top that hugs her breasts as they lean over a large cutting board. A group of teen guys that look just like members of Spencer's band, Ice Nine Kills, enter the house along with a large-chested brunette and another girl who appears to look much like Karen, the receptionist. The guy who looks like Patrick from the band—smooth, dark hair parted to the side, short facial hair, stretched ears, and two full-sleeve tattooed arms emanating from his white T-shirt—carries an orange cooler into the kitchen. The teen who resembles Julio, fashionably-feminine with spiked bleach-blonde hair and a black sleeveless tee, plops down two large handles of alcohol onto the counter.*

*The boy looks at the new arrivals before turning back to the window where he spots a shadowy figure wearing a blue one-piece jumpsuit and pale white mask with an "IX" on his forehead standing on the lawn. The boy looks away for a moment, calling over his babysitter to come and see the danger that he sees. When the boy looks back through the glass, the*

*Shadow Man has disappeared. The babysitter arrives at the window and scolds the boy for pretending to see something that isn't there. She walks away from him and he turns back to the window, noticing footprints leading toward the garage. Again, the boy tries to tell his babysitter about the figure, but she immediately dismisses him and promptly escorts him upstairs to bed. As the guys fill up the cooler with ice and alcoholic beverages, the large-chested brunette strips her clothes down to a blood-red lacy bra and panties. Karen does the same, removing her flowing blue dress to reveal a tight-fitting black bikini top and bottom. The teens run out to the hot tub to drink as the babysitter puts the boy to bed.*

*With everyone gone into the yard, or upstairs, the Shadow Man enters the house. He glides into the kitchen, quickly spotting the large knife set on top of the cutting board and wielding it as his own. The figure lurks in the back hallway leading to the garage for a moment before hearing the noise of one of the teens entering the nearby bathroom. The figure hides in the shadows of the corner at the end of the hall.*

*Fresh out of the bathroom, the teen that looks like Patrick strolls back toward the action. He walks down the hallway, flicking the lights off on his way, taking the secluded wing of the house from a bright orange to a dull black. Not a tick of a clock later, the figure descends on Patrick, placing his hand over his mouth, silencing any scream and slicing the knife horizontally across his throat with far greater ease than its previous user chopped her limes.*

*As she returns downstairs, Nancy, the babysitter, sees the outline of Patrick's body lying face down on the floor in the darkened room just steps away from the landing. She hits the lights, revealing a pool of blood oozing away from his gashed neck and toward the spot on which she is standing. Nancy lets out a scream worthy of curdling the blood that now gathered in front of her feet and echoing up the stairs to the boy and into the yard to the teens. Upon hearing her cry, Karen heads toward the house with Julio following, leaving behind the large-breasted brunette. Once inside, they reach Nancy as she continues to scream in terror, a contagious reaction that soon spreads to Karen and Julio. As panic sets in, Nancy attempts to call the police, but just as she hears a dispatcher on the other end, the lights and phone are cut off. The teens become sitting ducks, panicking and running in opposite directions in a vain attempt at escaping their fate.*

*Back in the hot tub, the lone brunette sits drinking her cheap beer and wondering what is taking the others so long. A stillness overtakes her, blissfully masking the horrors that lurk in the house, just a knife's throw away.*

*Meanwhile inside, Karen is left alone in the living room, Julio and Nancy have run off to find help nearby. Karen walks through the house, making sure that she is alone. She looks around a bit and sees no one. Suddenly, she feels a hand reach across her soft mouth. She gasps, struggling to draw in air just before a knife stabs down into her chest. Knife after knife, blow after blow, the blade rains down on her as blood splatters around the living room. Her body goes limp. The Shadow Man slowly draws his weapon out of Karen's chest, resisting the friction from her sticking blood. He then lurches his large frame toward the backdoor that leads to the yard.*

*From the rear door's four-pane window, he spots the lone girl, lounging in the hottub. He stealthily exits through the open door and makes his way toward her under the cover of darkness. Slowly inching his way through the crisp fall air toward his unassuming prey, the Shadow Man raises his knife in anticipation. Finally reaching her, he makes one swift motion where he springs from behind her and lowers his knife, sending a scarlet billow out of her neck and into the steamy water; her arteries rapidly draining their contents into the tub.*

"Hold on a second," the doctor interrupted. "I know time's almost up, but I just want to stop you there before I hear the rest. You never mentioned how things were going with some of these bandmates. They appear in your dreams in rather gruesome detail, but last I heard you were also having difficulty with them in real life."

"Yeah, let's just say a couple of them passed on."

"You mean they left the band?" Doctor Black prodded.

"Sure," Spencer replied, curtly. "We got a couple of new guys I'm really excited about. Dan Sugarman on guitar. His uncle was actually in *Friday the 13th, Part 2!* Very cool, as we're all such big horror movie fans. Also my good friend Joe Occhiuti, he's been playing in other bands that did shows with me since we were teenagers."

"Well that sounds promising," the doctor speculated.

"Definitely is. Patrick's still in, and then Ricky, who started back with us a few months ago and actually factors into this dream..." Spencer began, as he recounted the rest of the dream to the captivated doctor.

*Moments after the Shadow Man gutted Karen from breast to breast, a law officer with slick dark hair and a mustachioed face, resembling Ricky from Ice Nine Kills, enters the house. He briefly surveys the situation and immediately calls for backup through his shoulder-clipped radio. As soon as the officer finishes his assessment of the scene, a knife penetrates his back, sending him to the floor. Once there, the stabbing continues.*

*Nancy and Julio return to find the girl killed in the hot tub. Adrenaline heightening, they are desensitized to the brutality and their fight-response takes over from their flight-response. Knowing that help from the police is now on the way, they run into the house to find Karen and confront the horror that might befall them.*

*They enter through the back door and into the living room where they immediately see the bodies of Karen and a police officer. Any hope that they had for the arrival of help from the authorities, is immediately extinguished. Julio lets out a high-pitched scream and checks the bodies of Karen and the officer. As he bends down to have a look, the Shadow Man emerges, as if out of thin air. He again raises his blade and stabs Julio repeatedly in rhythmic succession, plunging his knife into his back again and again. The Shadow Man is so preoccupied with his current task that he fails to see Nancy has grabbed a poker from the nearby fireplace and swipes it across his head, sending him onto the ground. He loses his knife, which Nancy quickly dives on, snatching it up in one swift move. She gets onto her knees and moves over to straddle the Shadow Man, and she attempts to plunge the point of the knife into his chest. Before she can lower the blade, the man's hands reach up toward her neck faster than the blink of an eye. He wraps his hands around her neck, clenching them like a vice. She attempts to scream, but no sound or air escapes. With one last surge of energy she attempts to wrangle the knife into his body. The two tussle, moving left and right and shifting the weight of the Shadow Man onto the nearby fire poker. It penetrates through his abdomen, ending her nightmare, but not the dream itself.*

*The little boy, watching the entirety of the scene from the stairs, picks up the unattended knife and begins to emulate the stabbing motion of the Shadow Man. He smiles as his white T-shirt becomes splattered with blood.*

As the minutes passed and reached the end of their time, the doctor listened to the graphic detail of the dream as Spencer presented it, reserving judgement, yet pondering what mind could conjure up such horror.

# IV
## Savages

Jesse Kasem's voice echoed through the abandoned hallways of K-I-L-L Radio FM's station building. "Central-Texas' Home of Hard Rock" had just one rule that day: under no circumstances would they be playing any INK tracks. The calls poured in as fans all over the county sought to defend their favorite group. Was this just a stunt? Or were they really censoring these artists? Jesse himself fielded six such calls while Throat Yogurt's new single, "Two Inch Dick," languished on the air with its tired, stale sound.

Wearing his signature, patch-covered, black leather jacket and sunglasses, Jesse presided over the evening drive-time block, a slot he earned through his years of hard work in radio, slogging it out in backwoods towns all over the Midwest. He finally felt at home here in Kingston, TX, a small community, but one with a radio station that reached beyond the town's borders and serviced both the Austin and San Antonio markets. He loved it here and knew he would be in it for the long haul. He was confident enough in this fact that he had even bolted his favorite vinyl records into the brown walls of the studio, a sign of stability few DJs would ever show a radio station. He also liked the music he played. He even liked Ice Nine Kills, despite the new rule that they might be too extreme for the airwaves. Apparently the last time they had played their song, an old woman had a severe shopping cart accident out in Dowchester and the noise of the song playing nearby was ruled to have been a factor in the incident. The radio station settled for an undisclosed amount. Or so he told the listeners over the airwaves. That just drove them to call in even larger numbers. Little did those listening know that Ice Nine Kills would be played on the air in spite of the rules, and the fans calling in? They were about to have their thirst for INK satisfied.

Jesse flashed a smile and gave a thumbs up to his technician through the pane of glass that separated his booth from the control room. Sally, the wheel-chair bound A/V tech, braced herself, ready for what was about to happen. She had been manning some of the phones for the last hour, listening to countless rabid fans clamoring for their favorite band of psychos. With her wild hair and eighties aesthetic, Sally defined alternative. Now, she deftly wheeled her chair away from the phones and back to the controls. As the current song ended, she flicked a button, sending Jesse's voice back through the microphone and out to the people.

"We've got a special surprise today. In just a few minutes, Throat Yogurt will be performing here in our live studio! So be sure to tune in via our live stream and watch the video on our website!" He feigned excitement, imagining the boos that would confront him had his listeners been present. The band was terrible, and everybody out there knew it. He imagined they were only listening because of the new and unpopular rule they had created, and that was just where they wanted them.

Jesse watched as the band set up. It would be their third appearance in the studio in as many weeks; little did they know that what would soon occur would prevent the live concert from ever commencing. He checked the front door where Sally gave him a nod. "We've got just one track before the live show. So turn on that video livestream, because I think you're going to like this one."

Before he finished his sentence the sound of a chainsaw cut through the station and across the airwaves. Jesse looked up, immediately confronted with the image of the front doors open doors, sunlight pouring into the dimly lit studio, and from in between the shadow-casting members of INK. He clicked the song, "Savages" rang through the speakers and out into the world. INK was once again on the airwaves of K-I-L-L radio.

The lucky few who had tuned into the video livestream were seeing overhead footage of the studio and surrounding hallways. And, if they looked in the corner of the image, toward the front door, they would see the members from Ice Nine Kills standing in a row, ready for a takeover.

Clad in white dress shirts and brandishing an array of viscous weaponry, the band raised their weapons in unison with the start of the track. Red blood dripped down their faces and onto the white shirts, as Spencer, front and center with chainsaw in hand, had a scar slashed across his forehead and down his cheeks. Over his shirt he wore a leather apron, crusted with hardened blood, assumingly from a recent slaying. The other members wore various *Texas Chainsaw Massacre*-inspired memorabilia to accent their appearance: Patrick as the Sheriff from the remake, Ricky as the Hitchhiker from the original, and Joe as the imitable Chop Top .

They first took Sally by surprise, with Spencer firing up the chainsaw as she screamed over the track. She had forgotten to turn the microphone off, so the carnage would be heard through the radio for all those listening in. INK's Dan Sugarman, wearing a loose tie and sports coat that hung off his lanky body like it belonged to his father, cut his saw into the top of her head, sending a gush of red so far that it was hard to believe it could be real. He continued lowering his saw into her head, slicing her face in two as it split around his blade, laughing maniacally as he cut.

Choosing to spare the DJ, the band headed for the live studio, where Throat Yogurt was entertaining some young ladies as they awaited their set. Ricky burst in first, lifting a Kiss vinyl cover from his side and sliding out a serrated steel-edged record from the jacket. Everyone in the room was startled, screaming out as the band busted into their space. No one was caught off guard more than the crimp-haired bassist. Upon the band's entry, he abruptly received a steel record right between his eyes, splicing his forehead into two equal sections and sending his blood cascading over a nearby groupie. The record stayed lodged in his skull as he fell against the glass between the live studio and the DJ booth. Joe and Patrick double-teamed the drummer, sending him flying over his kit and onto the ground where they stomped on his limp body. In a stroke of creativity, Patrick stuck one end of a quarter-inch guitar cable into an electrical socket and the other end into the drummer's mouth, sending a final shock through his body that surely no one could survive. Dan grabbed a guitar and plugged it into an amp as the women screamed and ran to the other side of the room. One by one, the other members of the band replaced their counterparts in Throat Yogurt. Before grabbing the microphone, Spencer decided to sacrifice one of the groupies to the gods of music. Noticing a black guitar hook on the wall, he lifted a slim brunette in front of it before stabbing the hook through her back and out her front, splattering blood onto his face and chest. He figured the hook on the wall was not as decorative as a pair of deer antlers, but it would do the trick. Red blood oozed down her chin from her gurgling mouth as her legs kicked their last attempts at life. Finally, Spencer grabbed the mic, putting the whole band in place.

The song on the radio cut out and the band seamlessly took over, playing their newest single live as Jesse rocked out in the studio next door. Calls began pouring into the radio station, emergency services, police, even the FCC, as desperate listeners looked for anybody that could make the carnage people had just witnessed end. But it did not have to end, and the police had known about what would happen all along.

As Ice Nine Kills finished playing "Savages" live, Jesse got ready to go in and congratulate them on a job well done. One by one the members of Throat Yogurt, the groupies, even Sally, got up and cheered. They had all been in on the act: a large-scale stunt played against the fans and live-stream audience that nobody saw coming. Ice Nine Kills had returned to the airwaves in Central Texas and in a big way.

One week later, Spencer recounted the exact story as it happened to Doctor Ian Black in his usual therapy session. They had been holding such appointments over the course of the past couple of months, whenever Spencer was in town. The doctor sat wondering why this stunt was really necessary. He had no idea why the obsession with death and horror seemed to be such a central part of Spencer's life and his band.

Overall, the doctor worried that, as a boy, Spencer had endured a horribly traumatic experience, as detailed in a previous session's dream, but he could not connect it to a particular case. His research on Spencer from the past week had yielded only more mystery, as he was unable to uncover much. For all he could gather, Spencer had burst onto the music scene around the age of eighteen, with no discernable backstory prior to that. He did, however, find a similar case to the dream Spencer had been describing involving a young boy. The year was 1994. The city was Salem, MA, where Spencer supposedly hailed from. There was a mass murder that occurred in a home with numerous teenagers found dead and the lone survivor was a boy. No age or name was given, but Doctor Black was worried that it might be Spencer. The murderer was never found, but some authorities had thought it may be a man who later turned up dead. Unfortunately, none of the articles the doctor found gave a name to this man and, apparently, the police stopped pursuing the case after a while. Not wishing to further speculate on whether or not Spencer had been involved, the doctor tried some questioning about Spencer's present life in an attempt to lure an answer from his past.

In this current session the doctor thought he might start to get at what this obsession meant. He began with Spencer pointedly, asking, "Why do you have this obsession with death and destruction in your work do you think Spencer? This latest stunt might be something only a very twisted, very sick individual could come up with. Now, I don't think that you're sick or twisted, in fact, I reject those labels entirely. But I do wonder. Why all of the carnage?"

"It's all an act, you know? We just want to create a buzz," said Spencer.

"Well the chainsaw certainly helped you do that," replied Doctor Black.

Immediately picking up on his pun, Spencer replied, "I like what you did there, Doc. You know I'm a sucker for a good play on words!"

"Oh, yes. Well…" The doctor started, his face slowly fixing itself into a smile. "We can't be serious all of the time. I supposed that's what's happening here. Just a bit of fun and all that."

"You got it, Doc. It's all good, clean fun. That is, until someone loses a head," Spencer replied. He paused, before finishing. "Just kidding."

The doctor's smile fell, his face giving away his worry that his newest patient might not be taking their sessions as seriously as he had hoped. Perhaps he should try to catch Spencer in his everyday life to find the truth behind the image. He considered that fact that he might need to see him in his natural habitat to really understand what was going on. But that idea disappeared as his watch buzzed letting him know that the hour was almost up.

Spencer rose from the coach, letting the doctor know that he would see him the next week. He would be home for a short time between tour dates and would love to continue the sessions. Without saying so, Doctor Black thought that he might end up seeing him before next week if he were to try to observe Spencer outside of the sessions in some manner. As his patient headed for the door, the mystery became too much for him, and in that moment he decided that he would try to surreptitiously observe Spencer at home, perhaps later that very night. He watched his patient leave and began to furiously write his notes from the session while also recording some audio notes to himself to remind him of items that needed researching.

After he finished recording his account of the session, the doctor moved to his computer where he attempted to perform some of the research into the stories that surrounded his mysterious patient. Connecting the dots between Spencer's childhood trauma, his dreams, and the real-life tragedy that played out in Salem during Spencer's youth, the doctor wondered if things that happened in the real-world were somehow playing out in Spencer's dreams. Was it possible that maybe he was allowing news stories to influence his psyche? He decided to look into where Spencer had been on his recent tours, and whether or not something might have happened in those areas that could have caused these dreams. Certainly he had grown up in the Salem area, and the mystery surrounding the lone child from a crime scene intrigued him, but what about some more recent events? The doctor opened his laptop and began to search for anything that might have occurred around Spencer's tour dates and locations. He knew that Spencer had been through upstate New York and Texas, but was not sure of where else he had played; best to start there, he thought. A lot of the recent news coverage around New York was about a string of suicides in Upstate New York. A memory from his first time meeting with Spencer was immediately triggered. He had mentioned something similar in his dreams. Sure enough, the suicides had all happened around the time of Spencer's series of shows in that area. He used an Ice Nine Kills fan app, aptly marketing itself to "psychos only," to find the relevant tour dates. Spencer was in the area, but the connection was not clear. *How could suicides be a part of this?*

The hours passed and Doctor Black found himself deep in a rabbit hole of internet conspiracy theories mixed with legitimate news articles. Both of which had claims that the suicides were not, in fact, part of a pact—as local officials had said—but rather the work of a serial killer. While the authorities had dismissed these ideas, they were not without merit, as it did seem strange that the suicides ended almost as abruptly as they began, which happened to be right around the time that Spencer started seeing Doctor Black, and around the time he had left the New York area. He assured himself that this was purely a coincidence. However, what was less easily explained was a mass killing at a children's camp in Texas just a few weeks later. Spencer had been in that very area immediately after their first visit, on dates that coincided with this gruesome act. The doctor's suspicions were deepened. There was something about this patient that he could not put his finger on—a darkness. And, perhaps, here it was. He wanted to pay a visit to his colleague, Doctor Nancy Price, thinking it best that he get a second opinion on what the possible ramifications might be for not disclosing this kind of information to the authorities. Certainly it was not yet at that point, he still needed more evidence, but should he find another coincidence to corroborate these other two, it might be worth reporting. In the meantime, he was keeping detailed notes on Spencer, should it turn out that he was actually a killer, the doctor might be able to stake his career on it, maybe even get a book deal out of the whole thing.

Doctor Black got up from behind the computer, gave a stretch and small yawn, and started across the hall. Seeing Karen behind her reception desk, he was reminded that she might be able to help him gather more information about Spencer. "Still nothing from Doctor Michaelson's office about Spencer?" he asked her.

"No," she responded. "I tried them again twice today."

"I really need those transfer files, Karen. Get on it!" barked the doctor. He then gestured to Nancy's office asking, "Is she in?"

"She asked not to be disturb—"

Before Karen could finish her attempt to stop him, Doctor Black entered his colleague's office in the usual manner of knocking as the door was already halfway open. While it annoyed Nancy, she had learned to choose her battles.

As he burst in, Ian found Nancy between patients and taking a much needed hour for herself to read one of the trashy romance novels that she so very much enjoyed picking apart, dissecting it for all its poorly written glory; this was a favorite pastime of hers. She found today's selection, *The Sensual and the Savage* by Mary Fisher, to be particularly atrocious. Just as she reached a truly horrible passage, her officemate barged in, unannounced.

"Ian! You need to start knocking!" she shouted, lowering the novel and shoving it underneath her desk in shame. Her eyes began to blink rapidly, a tic that appeared whenever she was annoyed.

"It'll just take a second. I wanted to run something by you."

"What?" she replied, aggravated, but willing to entertain the distraction, provided it remained brief.

"Do you know of any studies done of serial killers *as* they were conducting their killings? Have you ever heard of such a study?" the doctor asked. "Because, I was thinking, almost all of the studies of psychotic killers were done *after* their killing sprees were concluded and the perpetrator was behind bars."

Doctor Price thought for a minute before she replied. "Well," she began. "Of course. No one could ethically study a murderer knowing full well...I mean...what made you think of this?" She became worried. "Does one of your patients present with—"

"Oh, no. No. Certainly not." the doctor interrupted. "Just reading a colleague's article and thinking how useful such a study might be. To chart how the psyche changes as each killing continues to mold it."

"Useful? Maybe. Impossible to conduct though. At least from any sort of *ethical* position. One would certainly lose their license that way."

"Of course, of course..." Doctor Black conceded. "Pity that though..."

"Weren't you working on a book about serial killers?" she asked. "What happened to that?"

"Ah yes, it was shelved for a bit, still not sure where it's going," replied the doctor, covering. "This question was more...theoretical in nature."

"I suppose the world would be better off knowing. But, still. Unethical," she replied. Considering the question answered, she looked down at her desk, eagerly awaiting the moment when she could return to reading. Doctor Black understood this action to mean he should depart, and taking his cue, he did.

As he crossed the hall back to his own office, he knew that he still needed the answers to his mystery. So, he decided, he would continue with his plan to observe Spencer outside of the therapy office. He needed to see where he went, what he did, and who he consorted with. This was an opportunity for him to conduct field research, just like in his college days. It excited him, and yet, he was also fearful of what he might uncover if he dug too deeply. Nevertheless, it was decided. He waited until Karen was gone for the day and checked behind her desk to find Spencer's file and retrieve his address. Later that evening, he would wait outside his home and see what kind of activities his patient engaged in.

# V
# The Jig Is Up

Hours after meeting with Doctor Price, Doctor Ian Black found himself sitting in his 2013 Volkswagen Passat outside of the luxury apartment complex occupied by his patient, Spencer Charnas. Having little field observation experience despite years of psychological research, the doctor relied on his knowledge of films to prepare for his stakeout. He had a mug of coffee, a sandwich, binoculars, and of course, something to do for the long wait that he would inevitably face (something often described in the films, but never depicted). For his distraction this evening, he felt it would be the perfect time to listen to some of the tapes from his sessions with Spencer and maybe go over a few of his notes. Perhaps he could make some headway in piecing together whatever might be lurking behind the friendly face of the musician. Of course, he had hoped there would be nothing there; and yet, he was unable to let go of the sneaking suspicion that there was a more sinister side to Spencer.

As Doctor Black was checking over the notes from Spencer's second session, he noticed the date in his notepad, a Friday in late August. Spencer had just come back from Texas. He wanted to replay the audio of Spencer's description of the dream, knowing that it connected to the real-life case he had read about earlier in the day. The easiest explanation was that this event was the impetus for the dream. However, the doctor could not put it out of his mind that it might be vice-versa. It was theoretically possible that Spencer was playing out his dreams in reality; it was possible that Spencer was a serial killer himself. The doctor became so excited at the notion that he spilled some of the James River BBQ Sauce from his roast beef threeway sandwich onto the recorder while he was attempting to pair it with his car's audio system. A roast beef sandwich from Nick's Roast Beef in Beverly, Massachusetts, had seemed like the perfect stakeout item, but the sheer volume of the sandwich became too much for one hand to handle and he had to reach for napkins to dry his device. He eventually paired it with the system and searched for this session record.

After locating the correct recording, the doctor soon heard Spencer's voice coming from his sound system. Spencer was recounting how, in his dream, he and a girl who looked like Nancy had barely survived a mysterious masked man. Just as the pair in the dream seemed home free, the man leapt up out of the water and attacked them one final time.

A church bell tolled in the distance and the doctor instantly became aware of how otherwise quiet the street was. No cars. Few people. Moments before, a woman in a gray coat had called her dog, Winston, into her house and now, another person wearing a hooded, black sweatshirt was smoking a cigarette while sitting on a stone wall across the street from the doctor. Other than that, the neighborhood had been deserted. Above the doctor's car a street light flickered: on, off, on, off. Staying off a moment. Then back on for good. He felt he should turn down the sound, worried that someone around might hear it leaking out from his car into the silence of the street. He lowered the volume just a touch then looked back down to his notes.

He was again lost in his thoughts for a while as, through the stereo speakers, Spencer continued to recount his dreams.

Eventually, Doctor Black looked back up and caught a glimpse of himself in the mirror. He was sweating. The heat was on too high in the car. *Had he been looking down too long? How long was he working on those notes?* He looked over to Spencer's apartment, or the one he assumed to be his. On the top (third) floor, corner unit, the first three windows on the right of the front of the building. The lights were still on. He hadn't left yet. Would he ever leave this evening, or was this just a futile pursuit? Doctor Black sighed with boredom and looked back down. Suddenly, he heard a: TAP, TAP, TAP.

The rapping at his driver's window made him jump, causing his notes to fall out of his hand. He abruptly turned down the sound from the car stereo upon his realization that the voice coming through his speakers was now reunited with the body, and Spencer's face filled his driver's side window.

"Out for a late-night drive, Doc?" Spencer questioned in a leading manner.

The doctor quickly rolled down the window. Then worrying that he had been caught spying, he stammered before answering, "Oh, Spencer! Hello..." He chuckled a bit, his nervousness betraying him.

"What are you doing here?"

"Oh...well...I have a friend who lives in this area. Just up the street actually."

"Just killing some time out here on my street, then?"

"You live in this neighborhood?" the doctor questioned in an unbelievable manner at best. "What a coincidence."

"It is, isn't it? Some might even say it's...hard to believe."

The doctor sat in silence for a fraction of a moment before Spencer moved. He tilted his head toward the radio and a quizzical look came across his face. He then lifted his leather jacket-clad arm and leaned over the doctor, toward the radio controls. While turning the volume knob up. Spencer asked, "Is that me you're listening to on the radio?" practically in the car with the doctor now as he reached over him.

The doctor was quick in his reply, stuttering a bit due to his mix of terror and embarrassment, "Why…yes!" he said, the words bursting from his mouth before he sheepishly continued, "sometimes, I listen to my case notes as I'm driving. What a coinkidink that it should be notes about you!"

"What do you know, another coincidence," Spencer retorted. "Well, it's getting late, you should probably head home. Or, to meet your *friend,*" he said, correcting himself. "This neighborhood, this time of night…it could be dangerous." As he spoke, a menacing tone entered his voice.

The doctor sat upright in his seat as the hair on his back pricked up. He became aware of his fight or flight response; he also knew which he would choose. "I'll bid my leave then," he said, his hand clumsily reaching for the keys to start the car. A nervous chuckle escaped his lips as he found the key and turned the engine over. Wishing to flee from the awkwardness of the situation the doctor was about to put the car in drive when he felt himself unable to depart without just one more question to his patient. "What are you doing out here, if I may ask?" he posited.

"You may, and I'll tell you. I was just having an old friend for dinner. Now on my way down to Gordon's Bar. Meeting another old friend of the Charnases. Family friend."

The doctor reacted quickly, not thinking about the words that would next leave his mouth, "Well, what do you know? Another coincidence. I happen to be meeting my friend there in just a few minutes."

"Well what do you know?" Spencer echoed.

"Is that all right if I go?" said Doctor Black. "I just mean, doctor-patient confidentiality and all…though, I can assure you that I will remain on the opposite side of the room and won't acknowledge that I know you. Or that you're a patient, of course. If it's all right with you if I even go at all."

"Sure, you can do whatever you like as far as I'm concerned." Spencer responded. "Maybe I'll see you soon then." He tapped the side of the door as he stood upright before walking down the street and toward the corner. The doctor watched Spencer as he continued down his street for two blocks. The person who he had previously seen wearing the black hooded sweatshirt crossed the street and seemed to follow him as he made a left two blocks down. He thought it strange but was unable to concentrate given the close call with Spencer.

Now that Spencer had turned the corner, Doctor Black breathed a sigh of relief. Now he would need to follow through so as not to be caught in a lie. He would have to follow Spencer to that bar and perhaps produce a friend as a cover. As he drove, Spencer's voice returned to the radio, describing one of his more recent dreams. It had featured a man seeking vengeance for his deceased wife. During this dream, Spencer felt himself die as well. The doctor found this to be curious and intriguing, as rarely does one die in their own dreams.

Doctor Black pulled his car just a few buildings past Gordon's Bar, settling into a space on the same side of the street. As he had never been to the establishment, let alone heard of it, he missed it at first, forcing him to do a lap around the block until he spotted it the second time around. Not knowing anyone else who lived in the area, he texted Nancy after parking and asked her to meet him at the bar under the guise that they needed to discuss their lease terms for the upcoming year.

Upon entering Gordon's Bar, the doctor noted that it was a particularly divey establishment, but did possess the charm of a place whose patrons frequented it for decades; it was, as one might say, an "old man bar." The decor consisted of a large mirror behind the dimly-lit array of liquor bottles, and bright neon signs that advertised beers-gone-by, illuminating the corners of the room. On the walls there was a collection of random objects, including a stuffed pig's head, a tiny bicycle, and what looked like a red and white Kabuki mask. The doctor noticed the upbeat ska music playing over the sound system, a song with a clever refrain about trusting a woman after her repeated cheating, the singer begrudgingly accepting that "she's the same." He had hoped that he could trust Nancy to meet him, as he would need that for his cover story to Spencer.

Doctor Black sidled up to the bar and slid onto the stool closest to the door, beneath a bright sign advertising "Strohmeyer's Beer." Behind him, an arcade shoot-em-up game startled him as the loud voice abruptly rang out, "Game over" as the player lost. He turned around to the young man in a baseball cap who had been playing, giving him a nod and a smile as he did so.

After stealthily searching around, he finally located Spencer, sitting in a corner booth at the far end of the establishment. Also in the booth was a shady-looking gentleman in a black hoodie. The doctor would be unable to hear any of his conversation and might need to use a well-timed trip to the restroom in that far end of the bar to try and listen in. He thought he would get a drink first, play it cool, and make his attempt later in the evening, perhaps even after Nancy had arrived. If she arrived at all, that was. He looked toward the door, hoping she would come in at that moment, as if by divine intervention, but found only disappointment.

Doctor Black sat for a moment, waiting for the bartender to acknowledge him. After a few seconds a bartender approached.

A hipster type in a knit cap and beard, he casually greeted the doctor, "Hey, man, what can I get you?"

"Oh, yes," started the doctor, forgetting that he was there to watch Spencer and not to drink. "Scotch, please."

"Any particular kind?" asked the bartender, his thick Boston ignoring the "r" in "particular."

"Something peaty, I guess?" said the doctor, unsure of himself.

"I got you," the bartender replied, turning around to search for the perfect bottle. He grabbed another. After he ceremoniously located what he was looking for, the bartender put a glass in front of the doctor. "How much do you want me to pour? Double?"

The doctor looked around, hoping to take a cue from what might be the appropriate amount; he had never been a big drinker. He saw a man about halfway down the bar who had a full glass of a brown liquid. "Less than him, I guess."

"Who, Jake?" replied the bartender in a whisper. "Yeah, I don't blame you, guy drinks like a fish." The doctor chuckled as the bartender filled his glass halfway. "I'm Larry. I own the place, let me know if you need anything." The doctor nodded amiably, having misjudged the bartender as being something less than the owner himself.

As he sipped his drink, he checked his watch, then the door, then his mark, Spencer. There was a conversation happening that he was not privy to. He decided to make a quick trip to the bathroom. He put his drink down and walked purposefully to the back of the bar, past Spencer's table on his right, and down a narrow hallway just a couple of feet away from Spencer's friend. In that back corridor, the doctor saw that there were two bathrooms, as well as a back door to the outside, through which he heard laughter and picked up the strong smell of cigarettes. He remained in the hallway next to an out-of-service payphone. From here, he would certainly be able to hear snippets of Spencer's conversation and hopefully duck out of the way should Spencer—or his friend—come into the hallway.

"Did you follow my instructions?" he heard Spencer say.

"Yeah, but...what do you even need all this for, man? Two drops should be more than enough to get you fuckin'—"

"What are you, my fucking therapist? Come on, Randy. You want the scripts? Or you want to give me a bunch of advice that I didn't ask for?" Spencer replied, producing Nancy's stolen prescription pad from his pocket.

"Hey, man, I'm just saying..." said Randy.

"Let's just say it's for someone who's getting too close," Spencer retorted.

"Oh man! Like a crazy fan? Awesome! I mean—"

"Yeah, like that..."

"Rock star life, man. So cool," said Randy, passing Spencer a vial as he did so. "All right, I'm out, but stay well, man."

As Randy got up, his back eclipsed the narrow passageway to the restrooms. The doctor flinched, worried he had been caught. He then slunk back toward the men's room and slipped inside just as Randy looked over his shoulder. He was safe inside the dingy two-person bathroom, hoping that neither Randy nor Spencer would be coming in to occupy the other space.

The bright fluorescent lights blinded him a moment as they cast their light into his unprepared eyes. Once his eyes had adjusted, the doctor saw that the place was filthy, water stains and muck everywhere, even what appeared to be a bloodstain in the middle of the floor. He declined to have a closer look. The doctor approached a urinal and unzipped his fly, figuring he might as well use the facilities while he was here.

He reflected on the conversation that he had heard moments before. He could barely make out the pieces of it, but knew that it had to do with some kind of crazed fan of Spencer's band. Perhaps she, or he, was giving Spencer stress, and, thus, was responsible for the nightmares. He finished urinating, gave a quick shake with the obligatory follow-up jiggle, washed his hands, and made his way to the dryer. He had to hit it a few times to turn it on and it was almost louder than the bar outside. He heard his phone ring as he was drying and had to maneuver quickly to answer. It was an unlisted number, but thinking little of it, he hit the green button and lifted the phone to his ear. "Hello?" he said, as he walked out into the bar area.

A German voice came over the speaker. "This is Doctor Ian Black, *ja*?"

"Yes, this is he. And with whom am I speaking?" He noticed that Spencer was no longer in his corner booth.

"*Guten tag*, this is doctor Zep Proyas from *Psychiatry Now*, Berlin."

"Yes, yes, of course," he said, cheerfully. He quickly realized that this call was more important than locating Spencer, and thus forgot about him almost immediately.

"Hello?" said the voice on the other end of the line.

"Yes. I'm here," the doctor replied. He waited a moment without hearing anything to continue. "You know, it's really quite loud in here," said Doctor Black, frantically carving a pathway toward the front of the bar. "I'm going to get someplace quieter. Won't be a moment."

"Yes, of course. Take your time."

As Doctor Black made his way to the exit, Spencer poked his head up from the booth he was sitting in, a cell phone to his ear. From outside the bar, Doctor Black once again engaged the caller, "Yes, I'm here. Still there?"

"Yes, of course, Doctor," said the German voice. "It's a bit loud where I am as well, no trouble."

From outside the front windows, the doctor could see his seat at the bar. "Well, doesn't sound that loud to me," he said into the phone. Through the window he could now see Spencer move toward the front of the bar and hover over the stool he had just left. "Now what can I do for you?" He watched as Spencer spoke to the bartender for a moment. "Oh, I know! Is this perhaps in response to the article that I had pitched regarding the minds of serial killers during their hunting? Because, I was thinking of turning it into a book, and, I must say, having an esteemed periodical of record such as yours would be the crowning achievement for my research—look at me, prattling on like an idiot. What did you say you were calling about? Doctor…Prius, was it? Proyas?"

There was no answer. He checked the phone again. It was disconnected. He had no way to call the publisher back. He cursed his bad connection and bad luck. Of all the calls to drop, why was it this one? He put his phone back in his pocket and returned to the bar. He would close out his tab and head home, hoping the caller would once again attempt to reach him.

Walking into the bar, Doctor Black heard a woman squeal with either pain or delight, he could not immediately be sure. Looking over to a front booth, he saw a young woman wearing a tight black dress flanked by two, young, punk guys, street-tough types in black leather jackets and T-shirts, one in a black knit skull cap, the other with a shaved head. She seemed to be okay as they hassled her. *All in good fun,* he figured. Besides, he was not the type to stick his nose into other people's business. Unless, of course, they were his patients. He reached his stool and sat down. Not a moment later, the men in the front booth playfully shoved the woman out of the booth. They headed toward the back of the bar and out into that smoking alleyway that he had noticed before.

After the group had departed, the doctor felt a cool breeze on the back of his neck as the front door opened. Turning around, he saw Doctor Nancy Price, dressed to kill, as always, this time in a long red coat and black thigh-high boots. She saw him immediately and walked toward him, greeting him along the way. "Ian, what is it? You sounded desperate for me to meet you here. What's going on with the lease?"

The doctor got off his bar stool and awkwardly greeted her with a kiss on the cheek. "Yes," he replied. "Well, I knew we had to talk about it soon. And I was here, in your neighborhood, and wouldn't you know it, but that Spencer bloke was here as well. I didn't want it to be too awkward, you know. Seeing the doctors outside of the room..."

"Why would you ask me here then? Why not just leave?"

"Well, I knew you lived nearby, you see," he replied sheepishly. "I just thought it might make us less approachable if we both were here."

"That makes zero sense, Ian. Can we just talk about the lease?"

"Of course. Drink? What'll you have?" he asked while finishing his previous scotch. Even though he needed to drive home, he figured one more couldn't hurt.

"Wine, please. White," she said, mostly to the bartender. He nodded his head and smiled flirtily back at her.

A few moments later, the bartender came over with the two drinks. "This one's on him," he said, pointing to the corner booth where Spencer gave a little wave.

The doctor popped some money on the bar to close out his previous round and began to sip his second scotch. "Aww, so nice," said Nancy. "We'll have to go over and thank him. So much for remaining in the shadows, Ian."

Doctor Black looked over at Spencer who was doing something on his phone. He saw him get up and go toward the back and into the outdoor smoking area. As he watched Spencer leave through the back, he suddenly felt light-headed. The room began to spin. *Had he had too much? It was only his second drink*, he assured himself. *Maybe he should visit the loo and sort it all out; some water on his face maybe? He might have just moved his head up too quickly to look at Spencer.* Thoughts rushed into his head as the blood rushed out.

"I'm just going to pop to the loo. Won't be a moment," he said.

Nancy looked at him as though witnessing a ghost. "Ian, you look really pale. Are you okay?" she asked.

He nodded his head and replied, "Yes, just need a moment is all. I'll be right as rain."

The doctor made his way toward the bathroom, stumbling as he went. At one point, he careened so far toward his right that he fell into a man on a bar stool. He managed to mumble a quick "excuse me," before continuing on. From behind him, he heard Nancy ask the bartender how much he had had to drink, but he did not hear the reply.

Finally, he reached the hallway to the bathrooms. He heard what seemed like shouting and crying from the doors leading out into the back area. Stumbling toward the noise, he put his hand on the door to the outside. A cool burst of air hit his face and he fell forward into the blackness.

# VI
## A Grave Mistake

*Doctor Ian Black falls through the back door of the bar and out into a small smoking area that has an alley leading away from the bar and onto the adjacent street. From the ground, he can see two large dumpsters to his immediate right, just in front of him. On his left, toward the alley, are the two men from the booth, forcing the same woman inside up against the brick wall of the bar. They grope her and try to undo the lace that ties her dress in the front. The one farthest away, with the knit skull cap, is shoving his hand up her skirt and attempting to finger her with his right hand, kissing her neck as she screams. As the doctor thumps onto the ground, the two men look down toward him. They are startled for a moment but laugh it off. The doctor is down on all fours, confused.*

*"You like to watch, old man?" asks the bald one, jokingly.*

*"Why don't you go home?" asks the man in the skull cap.*

*"Yeah, fly away like a scared little bird!" the bald man jokes. Both of the men laugh. The woman screams and tries to wriggle away.*

*"Good one, Bruce," the bald man says, complimenting his friend in the skull cap.*

*"Aww, what's the matter, Shelley? Is he your guardian angel, coming here to save ya?" replies Bruce, looking up at Shelley and removing his hand from her skirt.*

*"I don't even know this guy. Just. Please don't hurt him," begs Shelley.*

*"What do you care?" snaps Bruce. He pushes himself away from Shelley and the wall and turns toward the doctor. He takes two steps toward the doctor and then kicks him hard in the stomach. The doctor turns over onto his back with the force of Bruce's boot. He groans in pain. Bruce responds, "You made a big mistake, man. How are you gonna save her when you can't even save yourself!"*

*The two men pounce on the doctor, punching and kicking him while he's on the ground. He lifts his arms to defend himself, but the blows are more than he can stave off. The bald man drops to his knees and pins the doctor's neck down with his forearm, pressing so hard against his windpipe that he gasps for air. At the same time, the man identified as Bruce kicks him repeatedly in his ribs, painfully forcing air out through the pinched airway.*

*Suddenly, both men are pulled backward and yanked away from the doctor. "Run!" he hears a mysterious new voice say. The doctor falls over onto his side just in time to see Shelley running away down the alley and out onto a side street. He braces himself, wondering if someone else is about to attack him.*

*A face leans over him. It's a pale, white face, with black eyes that have vertical black lines drawn through them. The face's lips are also black. Aside from the coloring of the paint, the face seems familiar. He knows this face, but he cannot make it out on account of his swollen eyes that squint through pain and teardrops. "Spencer?" he whispers, his strength having departed from him during the beating.*

*"No," replies the man with the painted face.*

*It doesn't sound like Spencer, the voice is deeper, he thinks, but there is something familiar about this mystery man. The man turns away from the doctor and toward the attackers who are now bearing down on him, ready to attack.*

*From his vantage point on the ground, Doctor Black cannot see much, but he sees Bruce take out a switchblade and hold it out toward this man that looks like Spencer, who takes one look at the pitiful weapon and asks, "You really wanna take me on?"*

*"Maybe we should get out of here," says the bald man.*

*"Shut the fuck up, Mark," replies Bruce. "It's two against one. Get your knife out, idiot."*

*The doctor winces at the thought of weapons being introduced. He takes a better look and from the outline of the mystery man he is sure that it is Spencer, here to save him from these two bad men. His head swells and he is overcome by the same dizziness that he felt in the bar. He rests his head back on the pavement, obscuring his ability to see the fight.*

*After a momentary standoff, Bruce lunges toward Spencer with the knife. Spencer handily sidesteps the attack, leaning his body to his left and dodging the blade. He then steps back toward Bruce, grabbing Bruce's right arm in the process, and dexterously disarming him; the knife plummets to the ground. Mark lunges in an attempt to recover the fallen blade, but Spencer stops him with his foot, stomping it down on his open hand. Still holding Bruce's wrist, Spencer bends it back behind him before throwing Bruce forward, into the side of one of the dumpsters. His head bangs on the metal, which sends an echoing clang through the alleyway. Mark abandons his plan for the knife and gets up to run away down the alley. Before he can take a step, Spencer catches him by the collar of his leather jacket and pulls him backward toward himself. He then spins Mark around so they are face to face. Mark panics and tries to swing a quick punch at Spencer, but it is easily ducked. Without missing a beat, Spencer returns a punch of his own, landing it directly across Mark's jaw. Mark falls to the ground where he lays motionless for a moment before attempting to come into a crawling position. Spencer lifts his leg, raining it down on Mark in an axe kick, knocking him out cold. He then picks up the knife and stares at it for a minute as if remembering something.*

*Bruce then rises up, brushing off his jacket and adjusting his skull cap. He stands a moment before Spencer looks up from the knife and asks, "Not done yet?"*

*"Looks like we thought we could bring a knife to a gunfight," Bruce replies, as he pulls out a Smith & Wesson Model 629 .44 caliber magnum handgun. "Guess we were wrong. Won't make the same mistake again."*

*As Bruce raises the pistol, Spencer makes one swift motion that both moves him out of the path of any bullet that could be fired and also allows him to lunge quickly at Bruce from the side. The move is so fast that anyone watching, the doctor included, would believe that in that brief interlude, he took flight. Spencer uses a roundhouse kick to knock the gun from Bruce's clenched hand, sending the pistol clattering across the gravel. He then plunges the knife he is holding into Bruce's neck, splattering blood all over the alleyway. Out of Bruce's mouth blood sputters for a moment and continues to do so as his lifeless body slowly sinks to the ground. As he falls, Bruce's open eyes display nothing but emptiness.*

*Spencer stands staring at the scene for a moment while Mark gets up from the ground behind him. Unnoticed, Mark stealthily approaches Spencer. Careful to not alert Spencer to his presence, he slowly produces a butterfly knife from his pocket, flicking it open as he walks. Spencer hears him and abruptly turns around only to be met with Mark, who plunges the knife into Spencer's stomach. They stand there for what feels like an eternity, but is, in reality, just a few seconds. Mark cannot believe that he has actually killed a man. Spencer appears to be in shock as well. Then, as if by some magic force, he slowly pulls the knife from his own stomach showing neither fear nor pain.*

*"No. Please…" Mark begs, breathlessly upon seeing that Spencer did not die and now has the weapon. "I'm sorry. It was self-defense!"*

*Spencer plunges the knife into Mark's stomach. He does it again. And again. He is making sure that he has hit every major vital organ, removing all doubt that Mark will be alive when this is through.*

*Mark gurgles and stumbles back. He watches Spencer in disbelief, not understanding how someone he stabbed was unfazed by it in any way. He drops to his knees and slouches forward, doubling over as he crumples into a lifeless heap.*

*The doctor is watching. Realizing the threat is over and that he is saved, he turns over onto his back and looks up at the night sky. He sighs with relief, but as he does, he feels the acute pain in his sides from his injuries. Suddenly, the painted face of Spencer leans over him. He once again asks, "Spencer? Is that you?"*

*"No. My name's Eric," says the mystery man.*

*"Oh, well. Thank you," replies the doctor. "Whoever you are."*

*"You're welcome," says the man.*

*As he rolls over on his side in an attempt to get up, the doctor sees a woman in red approach. She takes Eric's hand and they walk out of the alley together just as the doctor's eyes close, and his body goes limp.*

"Excuse me, sir?" said a voice with a thick Boston accent. A pause, then the same voice continued, more harshly this time, "Hey, old man!" Doctor Black recognized it as the voice of Larry, the bartender. Coming to, the doctor blinked his eyes, before hearing the same voice again, scolding him, "Get up!"

"What?" he replied, groggily. "What happened?"

"You had a few too many and you missed the toilet by about thirty feet," said Larry, annoyed. He was holding a bag of trash, which he unceremoniously tossed into the dumpster before turning back toward his unwanted guest.

"Where are the bodies?" said the doctor, trying to pull himself up into a seated position against the wall.

"What bodies?" asked the bartender, detecting the familiar ramblings of a person who had a bit too much to drink.

"From the fight. There were two dead bodies." he said, still trying to get up, but wincing in pain.

"There ain't any bodies and there wasn't any fight. I'd have heard," the bartender said incredulously. "You're drunk. You need me to call you a cab?"

"I'm telling you, man, there was a terrible fight. Two men died! I was beaten up myself," said the doctor, lifting his shirt a bit to show horrible bruising around his sides. As he did so, he moved toward the green light illuminating the area near the trash dumpster. "Then he...someone... saved me."

"Oh shit," said the bartender, realizing his mistake. "Maybe I *should* call somebody...you don't look too good. Stay right there." He rushed back into the bar. The doctor collapsed, wondering to himself if it was all a dream. He looked at his phone. The screen was cracked but contained notifications of missed texts from Nancy asking him, *Where are you?* and saying she was going home. His eyes blurred and he could barely make out the words. He wondered if he had made it all up. She had certainly been there, but had he just drank too much and fallen asleep? Or did the events in his mind take place? He leaned his head back onto the brick wall of the bar, unable to hold it upright any longer, and fell asleep.

When he next woke up, Doctor Black was surrounded by EMTs and ambulance lights. Noise and commotion, sirens. Individual medics yelling various codes and instructions.

"Wait," he mumbled. "There were bodies here, I saw them... this is a crime scene!"

"Sir?" said a young female medic. "Sir, are you with us?"

"My patient. He's my patient! Spencer...but was he Eric...?"

"Stay with me, sir. You're going to be okay," the medic reassured. "Can you call this in? We need them ready," she barked to another medic, an older gentleman with salt and pepper hair and in peak physical condition.

"Sure," the older medic replied. He spoke into his radio. "This is Lee. We're inbound to you, male, sixties, portly, multiple fractures and bruises, may have drugs or alcohol in his system. Certainly under the influence of something…not making much sense. We're going to sedate him and get him in the bus."

"Was this a dream? Am I in a dream? Is it Spencer's dream?" the doctor asked.

"Man, I'd love to have what he's having," joked the older medic to the younger, who laughed.

"You're telling me, I'm the one pulling the double shift," she replied laughing along.

"But, if you'll just listen to me for a second!" cried the doctor. He was now strapped down onto a stretcher, his eyes fixed upward. As he saw the night sky disappear, replaced by the ceiling of an ambulance, he felt a cool liquid enter his veins intravenously. Seconds later, he was unconscious.

# VII
## Rocking the Boat

Doctor Black's eyes darted from side to side as he reread the television news ticker a second time, then a third. "Two Unidentified Men Found Dead: Hanged from Street Lights," it read. He knew these had to be the men he saw murdered. *Could it have all been imagined? It seemed so real.* He knew something had happened that night. After all, here he was, lying in a hospital bed, recovering from the injuries he sustained after being beaten nearly to death.

The hospital room was a bleak bluish-gray with wooden trim around the middle of the walls. To his left, the door to the hospital hallway and a small restroom with its doorway tucked just behind the main door. Directly across from the bed, a white board hung on the wall to chart his current vitals as well as which doctors and nurses were currently on-shift. At this time, the adjustable hospital bed holding the doctor was tilted to an upright angle, allowing him to more comfortably view the television in the corner of the room nearest to the window. Although he knew that he would only be recovering here for a short time, he had found himself bored of the monotony of his days. Nurses and the occasional doctor with their routine checkups were the only visitors into an otherwise television-laden routine. Other than that, he remained in his bed, bandaged around the sides. One of his arms was in a cast, while the other lay by his side with an intravenous tube leading into it. He no longer needed the breathing apparatus that had been intermittently used during the first few hours of his stay.

Now, on the third day of his hospitalization, the television finally gave him something to turn over in his mind with these news reports. Two mysterious men had been found dead from multiple wounds that were sustained prior to their being hanged from two adjacent street lights. Even more curious, authorities had discovered the bodies just two blocks away from the bar where the doctor had been beaten by two men. The news would not show the deceased, as is customary, but did describe the men as being in their early thirties and wearing leather jackets. These must be his attackers; it would be too much of a coincidence for them to not be. He wondered who had saved him then. *Was it Spencer?* Could he have served as both the doctor's savior and this mysterious hangman that now terrorized the city? The news was not reporting that these men were bad actors, but rather that they were mysteriously found hanged. This notion intrigued the doctor. It suddenly seemed possible to him that one man's hero could be another man's murderer. It was possible that Spencer could be both. Maybe this could be used in the book he was working on. This could be the angle.

Just as he sat thinking about the possibility of this idea, a knock came at the door and a late-twenties male nurse in dark blue scrubs entered. "Doctor Black? You have a visitor," he said. "Are you feeling up to it?"

"Sure!" replied the Doctor, excited to have some excitement for a change.

"Doctor Quint will be in with you in a bit, he's just starting rounds." said the nurse. "Probably be about an hour or two till he's here though. He takes his time."

"Sounds good," he laughed. He was unsure as to who might be visiting him. Nancy, maybe? He doubted that she would bother.

He had so few friends and none that might visit. As for family, he had just his two sisters, one of whom he had spoken to earlier in the day about visiting over Thanksgiving, and the other, who lived nearby, had stopped in on him the day before.

As the nurse left, Spencer walked in, flowers in hand. "Hey, Doc. How are you feeling?" he asked confidently, flashing Doctor Black a big white smile.

"Spencer! What a surprise. I'm doing all right. Considering…" He was shocked that a patient of his might visit, let alone this particular patient. Once again, Spencer had proven to be a surprise.

Striding over to a small table at the doctor's bedside, Spencer placed the vase of white, and blue flowers on top. "Brought you these," he said. "I'll just leave them here, if that's all right."

"Sure! Sure! Thank you. I wasn't expecting any visitors, let alone a patient. It means a lot, given everything else you've done, as well." The doctor said, hoping Spencer might admit to being the mystery savior from the bar. Seeing Spencer again, he was sure it was him.

"What do you mean?" asked Spencer, a sense of complete confusion was displayed on his face as he looked up from adjusting the flowers.

"Ah, yes. Yes of course." said the doctor, placing his finger on the side of his nose in a gesture of shared secret knowledge. "Say no more…"

"I'm not really understanding you, Doctor Black. Are you sure you're okay?"

"Never mind." said the Doctor, winking. He thought it best to change the subject and asked, "So, what made you decide to visit?"

"I wanted to make sure you were all right. Sounded like a pretty rough night at the bar. I apologize that I couldn't do more, I didn't realize you were…well, I thought you had left." Spencer said.

"Oh, you did quite enough, thank you," he replied. In response, Spencer nodded and smiled. After a moment of pause, the doctor continued, "I owe you an apology, Spencer."

"For what?"

"I believe I misjudged you. I thought, perhaps, you were something that you're not. Something bad. But you certainly turned out to be a hero, didn't you?"

"I'm still not following, but glad you feel that way," said Spencer, hoping to drop the subject entirely. "I had a nice chat with Nancy—er, Doctor Price, the other night. After we thought you left. Remarkable woman…"

"She is, isn't she?" replied Doctor Black. "Excellent doctor as well. I hope she's not fraternizing with you and treating you at the same time?"

"Oh, no. Of course not," assured Spencer. "I shouldn't need her anymore in the way of medicine."

"Ah, good, so you're not—?"

"But, I do need your services," Spencer interrupted. "I'm going to be away on this cruise ship tour for the next couple days, and then some other tour dates, but maybe when I'm back? If you feel up to it, of course."

"Of course. Oh, um, well…it depends on timing. I am intending to take a couple of weeks off," he said, gesturing to his bruised sides and holding up his arm. "Recovery and all? You understand. Just through the Thanksgiving holiday."

"Absolutely," Spencer replied. The doctor reached for a plastic cup of water that sat just out of reach on his bedside table. "Allow me," Spencer offered, starting toward the doctor as he did. He got his hand under the bluish-gray plastic cup just as the doctor's fingers slipped off of it, potentially sending it onto the floor if Spencer had not been there to assist.

"Thank you," said the doctor. "Another close call."

Spencer winked. "Always there in a pinch," he replied.

The doctor used his working arm to lift the cup to his lips and slowly sip the liquid. It was not particularly cool or refreshing, as everything in the entire hospital had the same lukewarm temperature and absence of flavor, but, nevertheless, it hit the spot. He had been thirsty for a few minutes, but thought it best to wait for someone else to be present and assist him in reaching the cup.

A youthful, pretty nurse with dark hair and wide eyes entered the room. She wore the same dark blue scrubs as the previous nurse and had red and gray sneakers. In front of her, she held a tray of food with a tinfoil covering. "Dinner for you Ian?" She set the tray down on a tall wheeling table with a wooden top that hung over the foot of his bed.

"Oh, yes. Thank you. What inedible offering are we choking down tonight?" the doctor replied, jokingly.

"It's supposed to be fish, but I'll let you be the judge. Sorry about the food, I'll try to round you up something else."

"I can grab you something," said Spencer, gesturing over his shoulder toward the door.

"No, no. Not at all. Thank you, though," replied the doctor, appreciating the gesture.

"Visiting hours are almost over anyways. Almost time to wash you, doctor. I'll be back in twenty," she said, turning on her heels and exiting the room.

"It's a sponge bath," Doctor Black whispered to Spencer, lecherously raising his eyebrows as he said it. "It's not all bad in here I suppose. Food aside, of course."

"Offer stands," said Spencer, pointing again toward the door. "For dinner, not a sponge bath."

"No, that's okay," laughed the doctor. "I do appreciate you coming in. Very nice of you."

"It was the least I could do," Spencer replied. "So where you heading? You said you were off for a couple of weeks?"

"Ah, yes," replied the doctor. "Colorado, actually. My sister, Wendy, runs a small bed and breakfast out in the country there. So I'll be visiting with her through Thanksgiving. I can stay at the inn, relax a bit. Good to get the outdoors a bit. Breathe some fresh air, and take some time away from it all after...well, after all that happened."

"Sure," consoled Spencer.

"It has given me some clarity, all of this. I've finally decided to begin writing a book that I've been putting off." For a moment he forgot who he was speaking with and continued, unencumbered by the fact that the potential subject of the book was in front of him. "Although, I'm not sure where to begin, as the subject that I was going to write about may not be panning out as I thought... eh, look at me gabbing on here like you're the therapist and I'm the patient." He thought about his words for a moment and then corrected himself, "not that you—or any of my patients—gab on about things! Hardly. It's all very enjoyable to hear, I assure you." Having almost disclosed too much to Spencer, the doctor began to stutter and stumble over his words, trying to get back on track.

"Don't worry," laughed Spencer. "I know what you mean."

"I think it'll be nice also to finally see Wendy as well. She's been in Colorado for the last thirteen or so years, so we don't get to see each other as much. My other sister lives just up the road, so I see her all the time. But it's always nice to see Wendy. It's quite a remote place where she is. A bit hard to get to, but worth it when you arrive."

"It sounds amazing."

"It is. And usually quite booked up this time of year, I'm told. Fall foliage and all. But I was quite lucky that she had a room available. She says she always has room for her favorite brother—I'm her only brother by the by—but, I know she'd sell a room if she could," the doctor chuckled. "She's an excellent business woman, and she really enjoys it. I guess this visit was just meant to be."

"Funny you'll be in Colorado. We'll be going through there too."

"I thought you were going on a boat?"

"Yeah, the boat sails out of Florida, we get off in Mexico and fly back to the states. Then we do a loop out to Los Angeles, through the Southwest, and end in Colorado. It's our annual Thanx-Killing tour, so we try to cover a lot of ground."

"I can see that."

Spencer's phone buzzed a couple of times indicating a text message. "It's nice to see all the parts of the country, though. Like you said, good to get some fresh air," as he replied, his eyes lingered on his phone, reading the screen. "Ugh, shit," he whispered.

"Everything all right?," asked the doctor.

"Yeah, just our tour manager, Jeremy," replied Spencer. "The guy's good. He's a real shark, but we're just getting so much pushback from these boat people. It's like a regular tour, but just happens to be on a boat, so there's a bunch of different bands and people get to see different shows, but also hit different ports, it's pretty awesome."

"Sounds wonderful," replied the doctor.

"And we sold out more than half this thing ourselves, so our fans are really excited," boasted Spencer, proud of the achievement.

"Looks like you're going to need a bigger boat," joked the doctor.

Spencer laughed before continuing. "Only thing is they don't want us doing meet and greets. Our manager Jeremy should be able to fix it, though. We say he has the power of the Schwartz.

That's his last name: Schwartz," Spencer replied, eliciting a chuckle from the doctor. "A huge part of our tour is meeting with the fans, the people that actually care about the music. This ship wants us to play our set and that's it. But, that's just not us."

"I can see how that would be frustrating," reassured the doctor. "Perhaps if you try to meet with the fans anyways, they can't possibly control all of your movements on the boat."

"That's not a bad idea. Maybe we can make it sort of a thing. Underground meet and greets where we give out last-minute, secret locations. Like a hunt."

"Does that make you the predator or the prey?" joked the doctor.

"Always a little bit of both," replied Spencer. "But I think you've figured that out." He tapped the doctor's left leg that was buried in the blankets. "I gotta get going. Glad to see you're better, you looked pretty roughed up after the other night." He spoke quickly and, upon finishing his sentence, was already out the door.

"Wait! How do you…?" he muttered. Then quietly to himself, "it was you."

# VIII
## Enjoy Your Slay

**Tuesday:** The Timberline Inn was just as he remembered it. Few details had been changed at the aging inn, even since Wendy had taken it over in 2006; it was still steeped in its late-seventies' aesthetic. Fortunately for Wendy, the design trend of bright yellows and oranges, contrasted against a deep brown, was back on-trend in the modern era, giving it a retro feel that some guests were sure to enjoy. Nevertheless, the elements of design did not interest her; her focus, and that of her typical guest, was the seclusion and scenic beauty of the property and its natural surroundings. The doctor also appreciated this aspect and got his first taste of it while riding with Wendy's husband, Sam, on the way from the airport. Sam was a big lunk of a man who seemed to be built for flannel shirts and puffer vests; he fit perfectly into his native state of Colorado. Being driven up through the evergreen-lined highway cut into the side of the Rocky Mountains, Doctor Black relished his chance to breathe in the fresh, albeit thin, mountain air. It was a far cry from the stale air of the hospital that he found himself in for a few days just the week prior.

The Timberline Inn property itself was up a winding road and afforded its guests a beautiful view overlooking a wooded dale, perfect for hikes. Sam pointed out each of these features to the doctor as they drove, making sure to comply with his wife's request of rolling out the red carpet for his brother-in-law, who, as he heard it, had had a rough couple of weeks. As they pulled into the parking lot, the doctor noticed the old-fashioned vacancy sign with its "no" lit up. Despite there being no room at the inn, his sister had still held a place for him, he concluded.

Upon arriving at the front entrance, Sam escorted the doctor with his luggage to the front desk. There, he saw his sister tending to a couple of guests who had just arrived moments before him. She flashed him a broad smile and a friendly wave, as well as an indication that she just needed one moment to help the elderly couple standing between them toward their room.

The lobby of the inn had high vaulted ceilings lined with dark wooden beams and large, south-facing, glass windows that overlooked the valley below. Much of the decorations were tapestries and paintings in warm colors that evoked traditional Native American design; the doctor found it to be reminiscent of his colleague Nancy's office. He had hoped for an escape from work, but something always managed to bring his mind back to it.

The inn had around forty rooms that could be accessed via two adjoining hallways exiting the lobby on the left and right sides. The guest areas were divided into three floors with approximately seven rooms on each floor of each wing. Like the front entrance, all the rooms faced south, offering an amazing view to each guest. A red-doored elevator was located at the front of each hallway in order to access the upper floors. Some of the rooms were larger suites, but most were double rooms with a queen-sized bed and ensuite bathroom. The inn was small enough to have only one restaurant and bar area but remote enough that it served a full menu for three meals each day to many of the guests.

Although they owned the inn, Wendy and Sam had an all-hands-on-deck approach to management. Thus, she was often found at the desk during the daytime hours. Wendy finished with the elderly couple before handing them off to the lone bellhop on the staff to assist them, and their luggage, to their room. Wendy then turned her attention toward her brother, whom she jumped toward and greeted with a big hug. She pulled back and looked at his bruises. "Oh, Ian. You look terrible," she said, half-joking. "But, you're here now. And that's what matters." Wendy's accent was not as strong as the doctor's but certainly had a tinge of her British upbringing. After pulling away from the hug, she quickly moved behind the desk and put on an overly business-like caricature of an innkeeper greeting a guest. "Now, Doctor Ian Black," she began, "let's find you your room." She turned herself to face an old-fashioned wall of keys behind her, and dexterously grabbed a key without looking; she had done this many times before and knew the precise location of each room's key.

Playing along with her act, the doctor responded, "Thank you very much, Mrs. Kubrick-Black. I must say you do have a lovely establishment here."

"Very kind, very kind," she replied. Wendy placed the key that she had removed from the hook labeled "Room 217" and placed it in Ian's hand. "Here you are," she said. "I figured you would appreciate the view, it's really our finest room."

"Oh, no. I couldn't," the doctor protested. "You shouldn't have—"

"Nonsense. It's all the way down at the end of the west wing. Amazing sunsets. Sam can take you there, but, so you know, it's the top floor, last room on the left. And after you're all settled in, we can do dinner up in our quarters. We're off the east wing, so down the other end. Sam can point that out too. He's sort of a jack-of-all-trades around here."

"More like a master-of-none," quipped Sam, sending the three of them into laughter.

"Somehow, I doubt that very much," said the doctor. "I'm glad to be back out here. This place still looks amazing. And you really are a sight for sore eyes, Wendy. It's great to see you." He lingered to stare at her just one more moment. As children, they had moved around so much, that his two sisters, and their parents, were all he knew of the concept of home. It was good to be back with her. Before they went toward the elevator, the doctor and Sam struggled over who would take the luggage, each insisting that they be the one to do it. In the end, Sam won out and he wheeled the doctor's roller bag away from the desk, the doctor following behind.

Moments later, they found themselves in the long hallway where Sam launched into some of the small talk that one does when seeing a relative that one is not particularly close to. "So," he began. "Wendy tells me you're here working on a book? Pretty exciting. I thought you were a shrink though? Dealing with crazy people and all."

"I'm a researcher and writer, primarily," he clapped back. "Or, intending to be. Seeing patients has been sort of a way of making ends meet." The doctor tried to hide his annoyance at the question, but it proved more difficult than he had anticipated. His answer also rang false, seeing as he usually enjoyed the fact that he saw patients. It had just become burdensome in the recent months for some reason.

"Ah, sorry, I didn't realize you had so many things going on. Sounds interesting," said Sam. He was kind at heart and made an effort with the doctor.

"No, no trouble at all. Sorry. Yes, I do love seeing the patients actually. I have some very interesting ones right now. One in particular has me always on tenterhooks. The book that I've been working on is intended to be based around his particular case. But, we'll see."

"Weren't you working primarily with the criminally insane? The real wackos of the world? Sorry, that's probably not the industry term."

"No, but understandable. And, yes, my primary focus has been serial murderers. And the book may touch on that."

"So this fella, he's a murderer?" asked Sam.

"Not exactly. Although, I suppose that remains to be seen," replied the doctor. Sam had stopped in front of Room 217 and the doctor followed suit. "Well, I guess I'll get settled in and then come call on you two. See you in a bit."

"See you soon," replied Sam. "And don't hesitate to call down if you need something. More than likely you'll get Wendy, or maybe Shelly, she comes on at five."

"Thanks," replied the doctor before shutting the door. He took a look around at the room. It was beautiful. Wendy and Sam had obviously redone many of the guest rooms recently, as this was much more modern than the rest of the hotel but still featured the same rustic charm. The carpeting was a hunter green and all of the furniture made of oak. The front door had a short hallway with an entrance to the bathroom on the left before opening into a living room area with a couch and television straight ahead and off to the right side. In that same main living room area there was also a small kitchenette. To the left side from the main hallway there was an entrance to the bedroom, which had a queen bed, and also had a second entrance to the same bathroom inside of it. Like the lobby, the decorations were Southwestern in style but much more modern in these updated rooms. A jackalope skull hung on the wall of the living room, coupled with a large orange and yellow tapestry on the opposite wall. In the far right hand corner of the living room there was a desk, which the doctor hoped would be useful for his writing over the days. This would be his home through Thanksgiving, and would hopefully serve as the creation site of his most important work, the book documenting his sessions with Spencer. Of course, the conclusion of the book could not yet be written, not until Spencer revealed his true actions and motivations. But, if Spencer turned out to be the serial killer that the doctor thought he was, the rights to this story could be sold for an astronomical amount, not to mention the publishing earnings. Of course, great advances in the psychological sciences would also be made by studying a serial killer while he was taking his victims. It went without saying that the doctor would go to the authorities as soon as he knew for sure, but for now, building out the structure of his book was of the utmost importance. This structure would help him find what the science was lacking, and hopefully, he could explore those areas within Spencer's mind to find the answers that had baffled psychologists for generations. Great work was to be created in this room, he could feel it in his bones.

**Thursday:** Doctor Black had dined with Wendy and Sam, as well as their eight-year-old twin boys, Danny and Tony, on that first night, and for the next two nights after. He used the days to begin some of the research portion of his project and to organize his notes with Spencer. Much of his research was on journal articles from other psychologists, as well as a few books that he brought along that easily fit into his luggage. Following dinner on that particular Thursday evening, he had excused himself from a wonderful Colorado lamb dinner, made by Wendy, in order to return to his room and write some more. He was researching a particular subset of serial killers that bragged about their killings, indirectly. This lined up with what he believed Spencer might be doing with the recounting of his dreams.

Upon returning to his room, he found himself particularly restless and was unable to concentrate on the task at hand. He instead chose to visit the hotel bar in the lobby that he knew would be open until only about eight o'clock but had a propensity to stay open much later if guests were still drinking. He looked over at the clock on the end table next to the couch and saw that it displayed the military time of 19:21, plenty of time for a drink. He thought back to the last time he had had any alcohol, weeks before. It was while he was at the bar where Spencer (or someone else, he was still unsure) had saved his life from the two street toughs who had jumped him in the back alleyway. Within the safe confines of his sister's hotel, he assumed that he would be able to stay out of such trouble.

Upon entering the restaurant, he saw that a lively crowd was gathered around the bar. The bar and restaurant was recently renovated, everything shining and new. It was a mix of oak wood on the tables, chairs, and bar top, as well as gold trim and accents. The bar area had a hunter green wallpaper that was similar to the walls in his room, while the restaurant was a shade of off-white with oak wainscot paneling coming halfway up the wall. The doctor sat at the far end of the bar on a corner stool and picked up a menu. He was stuffed from his meal with Wendy, but wanted to look nevertheless. He decided that he would order a glass of bourbon and was searching through the rows of bottles stacked behind the bar when he was approached by the bartender.

"What'll it be?" said the lanky man in a white dress shirt working behind the bar.

The doctor looked around behind the bartender for a moment. "I'll try that Grady Bourbon, is that any good?"

"Sure, it's local. So they say you can't really call it bourbon, something with those Kentucky folks, but we call it that anyways and it's damn good stuff," he chuckled. "You want it neat?"

"Rocks, please," responded the doctor.

"Hey, you're Wendy's brother, aren't you?"

"Guilty as charged," said the doctor, holding up his hands.

"Yeah, I figured from the accent. Name's Lloyd," he said, offering his hand for the doctor to shake.

"Ian," replied the doctor. His drink came and he took a sip, before asking "What do I owe you, Lloyd?"

"Your money's no good here," laughed Lloyd. "Orders from the house. I don't make the rules."

"Thank you. Or thank Wendy and Sam, I suppose," said the doctor before laying out a ten dollar bill on the bar. "Well, that's for you, nevertheless."

"Hey, if you like, you can just take this bottle up to your room," suggested Lloyd. "It's good stuff."

"Oh, I, uh...Are you sure?" replied the doctor. Then, after thinking a moment. "Well, I suppose, if you insist. It is quite good."

After the doctor sipped his drink a few times, the man at the next stool leaned over to him. He was an older, African-American man of about seventy years of age, he had short-cropped white hair and a raspy voice as he spoke. "You know I couldn't help but hear that you're Wendy's brother. What a lovely woman."

"Yes. You know her then?" said the doctor.

"Of course, of course. My wife and I have been coming here for years. We just love it. We're from Miami, you know. Quite the change in weather for us. Usually folks go the other way for winter," he laughed.

"Ha, yes," chuckled the doctor. "I'm Doctor Ian Black, or Ian, nice to meet you."

"Hey now. A doctor? Don't get me started on what I got wrong with me, we could be here all night," said the man, laughing uproariously at his own joke. "Name's Dick, and if my wife asks, you never met me." He continued laughing, slapping his knee in excitement. "Reminds me, though, I better finish this and get back upstairs. She's probably asleep by now, so the coast is clear." He laughed again, before drinking down the red, tropical-looking liquid in his glass, sighing with satisfaction as he finished. "Ahh, that was all right. You outdid yourself, Lloyd. What'd you call that? A Red Rum?" Lloyd nodded. "That's some good stuff. You can take the man outta Miami, but you can't take the Miami outta me."

The three laughed at his quip and Dick got up off the bar stool. Doctor Black enjoyed meeting happy people, he had not had a really good laugh in months, he realized, and the feeling was strange. He wished this new pal of his would not be disappearing so soon. "Yes, well, very nice to meet you and I'm sure I'll see you around," said the doctor.

"Oh, I'm sure you will, Doc. You take care now." Dick waved goodbye and left the room.

After a bit more time in the bar, the doctor finished his first glass. He decided to call it a night but brought the bottle up to his room. He attempted to write for a bit but found it difficult; he simply lacked the motivation. Instead, he had a glass or two more of bourbon and called it quits.

**Saturday:** The doctor had been working at his writing for days now but found it nearly impossible. He had, however, spent quality time with his family. They went on hikes through the surrounding hills, and he watched the sunsets shine through his window in the evenings. He also had plenty of time to write, which, nevertheless, proved unfruitful, given that he could not grasp precisely what it was that he was writing about. There was still so much of Spencer's life that the doctor remained in the dark about.

On the Saturday of his first weekend, he had been on a hike with his nephews when they came across a dead rabbit in the middle of the trail. Tony seemed particularly fascinated by the body, poking it with a stick, then using the stick to draw a line in the freshly-fallen slow using the partially-frozen blood that had leaked out of the carcass. Tony's fascination did not strike Doctor Black as being particularly alarming behavior; it was typical for boys his age to marvel at such things. However, he became increasingly concerned when the boys showed him a clearing in the woods where there were no less than twelve dead rabbits scattered about, their bodies partially mutilated with much of their remains left intact. The doctor gasped, Danny shut his eyes, unable to look at the horror before them. Tony, however, looked on with amazement, maybe even a sense of accomplishment. The doctor noted this and intended to ask Sam and his sister about it later at dinner. If Tony had killed all of these rabbits, this would be a troubling fact for the doctor. He knew that all too often an early sign of a future serial killer was the mutilating of animals; he was now worried about his nephew.

**Monday:** Doctor Black again found himself dining with his sister and her husband, as well as the boys. They had not eaten together the two nights prior as there were a lot of new check-ins at the inn over the weekend requiring the full attention of the two owners. Instead, he ate in his room the first evening, and in the bar the next. At the bar, he was fortunate enough to have another chance to talk and laugh with his new friend, Dick. He even met Dick's wife as she came down to yell at him to get back upstairs after he had stayed long past the dinner hour and continued to drink with the crowd.

On Monday evening, however, Doctor Black once again returned for supper to his sister and brother-in-law's apartment at the end of the east wing of the building. The rustic look of their farm-like kitchen was tastefully crafted, and the beautiful oak table at the center fit the room perfectly. Newer appliances amidst the older cabinetry, showed the couple's ability to balance an appreciation for historical architecture with a desire for modern conveniences and its technology.

The apartment as a whole, however, had the messiness that would accompany twin boys who had two working parents with demanding schedules, but that simply gave it character in the eyes of the doctor. It also made him feel as though something was missing from his own life. His house and office were certainly as messy as Wendy's home, but for him, the excuse that comes with children was missing. Of course, children were not just an excuse for being untidy. They also held a greater, societal purpose: the idea of the Black family name living on for generations to come. Having just two sisters, he would be the sole opportunity within their family to continue the lineage through a male. He was worried that he may never have children, and spending more time with either of his sisters, both of whom had children, only deepened that fear and worsened that regret.

After the meal was finished and the boys went back to their room to play, the doctor felt it was the best opportunity to raise the delicate subject of Tony and the rabbits. He had felt the nagging pain in his gut throughout the entire night as his stress levels elevated prior to having this conversation. However, having had three glasses of wine with dinner, he now felt lubricated enough to hold such a discussion. Although he knew that his sister would respect his opinion as a psychologist, it was difficult to give advice or negative feedback to parents about their children; this was further complicated when the parents were, themselves, a part of one's own family. At least now the alcohol could do some of the broaching of the subject for him.

"I was out walking with the boys the other day," the doctor began. "And I came across a most peculiar sight."

"Yeah?" replied Wendy.

"There was a clearing off the path that leads deeper into the woods and down into the valley. To the right of the front entrance."

Sam started laughing. Half of a chocolate chip cookie was visible inside of his mouth. "Oh, yeah. They showed you," he said, finishing his bite between phrases.

"Yes?" replied the doctor, a mix of shock and concern visibly displayed in his face.

"The rabbits, right, Ian?" said Wendy.

"Yes, the rabbits. Aren't you the least bit concerned? My work has shown me that—"

"What would this have to do with your work? Have you gotten into veterinary sciences?" asked Sam, attempting to make a joke.

The doctor replied in a whisper, gesturing to the boys whom he did not want to be within an earshot of, "No, the work with the serial killers. And I'm not saying that they are—maybe they saw it on television?"

"Ian, what are you talking about?" said Nancy, astonished. "What did the boys tell you?"

"Nothing, their looks said enough. Tony's in particular. I like to think that after years of studying these kinds of people, that I—"

Sam cut him off, "What kinds of people? Killers? You think that our boys are—"

"No. no. I'm not saying that at all. It's just that sometimes the mutilation of animals can be an early indicator of much deeper and more serious problems to come."

Sam scoffed, turning to Wendy. "Mutilating ani—? Is he serious? Mutilating animals?"

"Ian, there's been a rash of rabbit deaths due to an outbreak of some disease," Wendy elaborated.

"A disease? But, I saw them. There was blood, they were mutilated," insisted the doctor.

"Turkey vultures. They eat them on their way south," said Sam. "Only, they get a whiff of these guys and realize they got something wrong with them, so just kind of move on after a bite or two."

"See, Ian? Nothing to worry about. No big, scary, serial killers out here," laughed Wendy. "Just two little terrors of our own, tearing up the apartment and nothing else."

"Yes, well. I'm terribly sorry," muttered Ian, stumbling over his words. The recurrent stabbing pain swelled in his stomach and fixed itself around his liver area. "I didn't mean to insinuate that—I was merely suggesting that, perhaps..."

"It's all right," offered Sam. "You've seen some horrors I'm sure. But it's a quieter life out here, as you can see. Nothing like in the movies."

"Well I don't usually watch those types of—yes, yes, of course. Again, I'm very sorry to have even suggested that the boys were in any way responsible. Perhaps I've been too focused on this book, trying to make things exist, when they really don't."

"It's fine, Ian, we're just winding you up," Wendy reassured him. "You thought our kids were serial killers. Or just one kid, I guess. As if they didn't do everything together." She and Sam laughed, and Ian joined in soon after. "Now, Ian, you do understand that Sam and I can never let you live this down? This will forever be the day you decided Tony was a serial killer." She had attempted to be serious through the previous phrase but found herself breaking into laughter before she could finish.

They sat for a bit longer and enjoyed each other's company. The doctor, still feeling embarrassed about the entire situation, repeatedly apologized for his mistake. It worried him that he may be seeing things where they didn't exist. Perhaps he had also done this with Spencer, he thought to himself while on the lonely walk back to his room. He decided to skip the writing for the night and instead chose to see what he might find on the television, which eventually ended with little success and his falling asleep on the couch.

**Wednesday:** The phone felt like it was ringing inside of Doctor Black's head. He had passed out just a few minutes past ten, having drunk the rest of the bottle of bourbon from the other night, and then starting a second bottle, but this time, it was of Jack Daniels. He had not anticipated drinking so much, but his inability to write his book about serial killers and fit Spencer into the center of it pushed him further down the bottle each day. The hotel room phone was set to be loud enough for a wakeup call, and while he was being given one now, it was not something he had ordered, and certainly not at this hour. It was almost eleven o'clock, he had not been out long enough to sleep off much of the booze.

The doctor reached toward the phone and managed to knock it off its cradle and into his hand. "Hello," he answered loudly, attempting to push the sleep out of his body using the strength of his voice.

"Doctor Black?" said a female voice on the other end.

"Yes? Who is it?"

"This is Shelley at the front desk," she said, urgently. "We have an emergency situation, could you come down as soon as possible?"

"Yes, of course!" replied the doctor, springing out of bed. He put on the robe and slippers that were provided for him in the room and took his key before exiting the room and shuffling down the hall.

Upon arriving in the lobby he found that it was quiet, most people had gone to bed, but a commotion was stirring in an area between the front desk and the restaurant. As he approached, he noticed a man on the ground, unconscious, with a few guests and staff members gathered around. After he got closer, he could see that the man on the ground was Dick, his new friend from the bar.

"Doctor Black!" said a young woman whose voice he recognized from the phone call that woke him up. She spoke with panic in her voice. "I didn't know who else to call. But I saw you're a doctor and I know you're Wendy's brother, so I figured you might be able to help. He's not breathing and I called an ambulance, but they're ten minutes away."

"I'm not actually that kind of doctor…" said Doctor Black, still waking up and confronted with the horror of his new friend lying on the ground.

"Can you do something?" said Shelley, recoiling from the smell of whiskey that emanated from the doctor.

"I suppose I can try. Has anyone begun CPR?"

"No, not yet," said Shelley. A few other guests came down from their rooms, perhaps hearing the commotion.

"It's been so long since I did this," said the doctor, kneeling down. "Does anybody else here know CPR?"

A woman in the crowd stepped forward. "I do. I'm certified, maybe I can help."

"Yes, certainly," replied the doctor, standing back up with some difficulty. "You would know better than I would. As I said, I'm really not that kind of doctor. I deal in the mind, and, uh…yes, well." The doctor stumbled over his words. He stood and watched for the next few moments as the woman performed CPR on Dick, who remained unresponsive. She kept it up though, hoping to maintain his blood flow at least until the ambulance had arrived.

He felt the eyes of the other guests fixated on him, watching his shameful moment. Sam and Wendy had also arrived. The look of disappointment on Wendy's face as she talked with her brother was enough to make him feel even worse than the hangover he would undoubtedly have the next morning.

Eventually, the EMTs arrived. As if by some miracle, Dick was revived using a defibrillator. The doctor did not believe in such things as miracles and knew it to be medical science that kept this man alive; if only he had been able to help, rather than simply standing around drunkenly gawking at the scene. Apparently, Dick had heart trouble and was not supposed to be drinking. The doctor watched as Dick's wife berated his newly resurrected self for being down in the bar rather than upstairs asleep. Despite the dressing down, Doctor Black envied Dick. He had a loving wife that cared for his well-being; he wished in that moment that he had someone to yell at him, someone to whip him into shape. Instead, he returned alone to his room, cursing the uselessness of his psychological degrees to save lives and longing for someone who loved him enough to loathe him as much as he loathed himself.

**Four p.m., Thanksgiving Day:** The meal was magnificent. Wendy really was excellent in the kitchen, and Sam was certainly no slouch either. Together, they whipped up a meal fit for royalty, and like the succulent, golden-brown turkey at the center of the table, the doctor was stuffed by the end of it. It was just what he needed to forget the events of the previous evening; rarely had he felt so helpless as he did watching Dick practically dying on the floor in front of him.

After the meal, the family gathered in the living room for what Sam assured the doctor was even more traditional than turkey: watching football. Never a man for American sports, the doctor found it a bit difficult to follow but nevertheless enjoyed the pageantry of it all. At what the doctor understood to be "halftime," the broadcast was interrupted. The KDK Channel 12 News team cut into the broadcast with a somber report of a mysterious string of murders happening across the Southwest and into Colorado. It seemed that his work could never let the doctor have a day off. Not that he would need to go and assist, certainly no one was seeking him out for his opinion in a case like this. Rather, the wheels in his mind began to go to work, wondering if somehow, someway, Spencer had anything to do with the report that he was witnessing. The first murder occurred the week before in Torrance, CA. From there, a succession of potentially connected killings spanned three states, and today, a fourth, Colorado.

It was certainly possible that if Spencer was touring in the Southwest, he could have been involved. Doctor Black now had the Ice Nine Kills app on his phone and he quickly started pulling up tour dates while also listening to the report. It was a stretch to think that Spencer could play his shows and kill all of these people at the same time, but still worth checking into.

The bodies were found in succession, moving west to east, with the first being discovered in California and laid out in a crucifix-like position. At first, this fact had led the police to think that it was some kind of religious murder. However, over the course of the week, they had discovered other mutilated bodies, each in a different location, and each spelling out a different letter through the creative use of limbs and torsos. This led the first body, originally thought to be laid out in a cross, to be reclassified as forming the letter "T." The next body found, also in California, was in the shape of the letter "H," then bodies in an "A" and an "N" in Nevada. By the time the authorities found two bodies in the shape of the letter "K" in Arizona, they feared that the entire word of "THANKSGIVING" might be spelled prior to that upcoming Thursday. Instead the bodies had all been found in the span of three days and had seemed to stop, until today. What made this news of particular interest to the Colorado area was that another body had just been found. It was laid out in the shape of an "S," its arms and legs broken, then bent, to make the perfect curve, and it was discovered just outside of Denver. Only a couple hours from where the doctor was at that moment. His heart sank, worried that maybe Spencer was on a killing spree that was heading right for him. He calmed down as he reasoned that this might be too far-fetched, and besides, Spencer would never kill him, the doctor was helping him.

The FBI became involved when the case spread out of California and law enforcement thought that they might be dealing with a serial killer that was crossing state lines to send a message. The message, as it stood for now, was "THANKS." Dubbed the "Thanksgiving Killer," whomever was behind this had baffled authorities and there was little hope of catching the person given the large swath of ground they had covered.

Doctor Black knew that many serial killers could go undetected for years, even decades, before anybody caught up to them. As the football game returned to the broadcast, he wondered silently to himself if he might be of some help in this case. The doctor took out his phone and looked up the Ice Nine Kills tour dates. It seemed that Spencer had played shows in each of those states, but relatively far away from where the bodies were actually found. In order to have been involved, he would have had to drive like a madman to get from one location to another. This was particularly true for Nevada, where a body had been discovered in Reno the previous Saturday evening. Spencer had played a show that same night in Las Vegas, almost ten hours away. Still though, the notion was intriguing to the doctor.

The doctor returned to his room after the game had ended and continued to question whether or not Spencer had been involved. He worried his sister and brother-in-law may have noticed that he was suddenly distanced, but he blamed it on the big meal and they said nothing more. He was researching Spencer for a while, trying to understand him a little better. He watched some footage of his shows, interviews, and even looked into the band members surrounding Spencer, as well. One interesting piece that struck him was the mysterious disappearance of a particular member of Ice Nine Kills, JC. After researching the case, the doctor found it curious that the search for him had been abandoned, and his status within the band declared as being "on hiatus." He wrestled with whether or not he had enough to go to the police, given that people were disappearing even from within Spencer's tight-knit circle.

It was in the moments before he went to sleep for that final night in Colorado that the doctor decided that Spencer warranted further study before he made any rash moves by complicating the situation with any type of law enforcement. Spencer may have been innocent, he reasoned, and it could just be one big coincidence. At least, that was something he could tell himself so that he could rest comfortably that night. Deep down, however, he knew the real reason that he was not going to the police was his own ego. The doctor knew that concurrent treatment and observation of a patient by a psychologist, while they are conducting their serial killings would be of the utmost importance to the field of study; and he hoped to be the first doctor to do it.

He flipped on the television and came across a horror movie, the type of film that he knew Spencer had enjoyed watching. He had always thought the genre to be tasteless filth, gratuitous in gore, and utterly lacking in any redeemable quality, not to mention the grotesque exploitation of women. He drifted off to sleep while watching the film and simultaneously thinking of the bodies that were found around the Southwest. His dreams became infested with this "trail of fears," as the news had so tactlessly put it. Much like his patient, the doctor was now finding himself plagued by horrific dreams. However, unlike those belonging to Spencer, the doctor's dreams could not possibly be construed as a confession; they were merely a processing of recent events. The dream on this particular night allowed his subconscious to answer a big question his conscious mind had posed: if Spencer had done it, *how* did he do it.

# IX
# Freak Flag

As the doctor slept, visions of a killing-spree that Spencer may have committed raced through his mind like the Ice Nine Kills tour bus most assuredly raced across the southwestern portion of the United States. Unaware that his subconscious mind was behaving in a strange manner, the doctor experienced a dream much like those of his patient.

*Ice Nine Kills are playing a show in a large, outdoor venue. The area is in a desert climate, hot and arid. Fans crowd toward the stage, clamoring for a closer view of their favorite band and kicking up dry, tan-colored dirt, which gathers into little clouds as they press forward. The band's set ends and they and their crew load up into a black tour bus with red and white lettering of the band's name. Two red and blue flags that say "Ice Nine Kills" stand straight up on their poles flanking the driver's cabin of the bus. While the band and crew do a mix of loading up and hanging out, they start to crack open beers and mingle with fans who come by the bus. Spencer, however, is nowhere to be found. Instead, he has left the area in a separate car. It's a vintage, 1970s Cadillac Eldorado, a long-bodied boat of a car with a convertible top. He drives off while the rest of the band is still at the festival grounds of the show.*

*Later that day, the sun sets over a now-empty field. Matted-down, dead grass is punctuated with the occasional stage, flanked by large amplifiers, and dotted with steel barriers for crowd control. The tour buses roll out one-by-one. The INK bus is still there, but no sign of Spencer's Eldorado. Instead, his bandmates pace angrily in front of their large vehicle, waiting for their front man so they can move on to the next tour date. As they wait, the band's tour bus driver, Otis Spaulding, sneaks a shot of whiskey from a flask. He is lanky and unkempt, rough around the edges, with greasy gray hair springing from his thin skull around the bald patch on top of his head.*

*Finally, Spencer rolls up, sunglasses on and his arms exposed by a sleeveless T-shirt reading "Dahm and Dahmer" that the doctor had seen him sporting during one of their sessions, noting the reference to the serial killer and confirmed cannibal. Spencer gets out of his car and walks over to his bandmates. JC, sporting a reddish-blond beard and donning a black T-shirt and sunglasses, is the first to notice that Spencer has returned.*

*"There you are, I've been calling you for like an hour," says JC, gesturing for Spencer to follow him to the far side of the bus. As they walk, JC hands Spencer an all-access pass for the next day that matches the one JC wears around his neck. "Where the hell have you been?"*

*"My phone died," replies Spencer, matter of factly.*

*Noticing that Spencer's hand is bandaged up and bleeding through its wrapping, JC gestures toward it. "What happened to you? What's this?"*

*"Don't worry about it. It's not even worth explaining," Spencer says, dismissing him entirely. Before he pulls his hand away, JC sees that it is both red with blood, and black and blue with bruising, covered in a white gauze; it looks like an American flag made of pain.*

*"Wait, wait," insists JC, standing in front of Spencer as he attempts to walk away.*

*"Come on, let's go." As he speaks, Spencer breaks free and starts toward the other side of the bus.*

*Refusing to drop the issue, JC continues, "Is this something I gotta worry about? What is this?"*

*"Something to worry about? What the fuck do you mean?" snaps Spencer.*

*"Showing up late, leaving? Sneaking off early?" asks JC. "Since when do we, like, keep stuff from each other?"*

*"Your mind goes to the darkest places," Spencer responds, placing his arm assuringly on JC's shoulder. "Okay, my phone died, and so I couldn't answer it. If there's anything more to it, I would tell you, but we got a ten hour drive, let's get the fuck out of here. Tell Otis he can be the captain, he's got the lead, we can trailer my car and I'll ride with you guys to Albuquerque tonight."*

*"Okay. Thank you," JC concedes. He nods at Spencer in agreement and then walks away to find Otis. Spencer, meanwhile, prepares his car to be towed by the bus so that he does not need to drive it.*

*Hours later, the bus having made its way across I-40 East, they all arrive at their destination: Albuquerque. While en route, a couple of the band members played instruments and sang along with roadies and groupies, while the others took the chance to nap. They all pitch in to unload the bus and relocate their belongings into a motel for the evening. Spencer has the crew drop his car down off the tow hitch so that he can go out and get some late night food; he claims to have a hankering for their famous green-chile burgers.*

*Later, Spencer returns to the motel, where the band and crew are partying with a large group of people in the parking lot as well as many of the rooms. Beers are flowing and music is blasting. There are a few other bands staying in the same motel, including the all-female group, Banjo and Sullivan, and they have joined in on the fun. Spencer opts to join the party and mingle, figuring he might find something, or someone, that he is looking for. He strikes up a conversation with two of the women from Banjo and Sullivan and convinces them to accompany him back to his room.*

*Once in the safety of his nondescript motel room, Spencer gets a better look at the two women. Both are petite, one is blonde and the other brunette. They both look like they could easily fit in at Coachella or another type of trendy festival. The blonde, Gloria, is dressed in a red crop top and straw cowboy hat, and short, Daisy Duke jean shorts that ride up, tightly cupping her backside as they do. The brunette, Winnie, has big, brown eyes and wears a blue bandana shirt over her waifish torso, hugging her pert breasts. Spencer begins to kiss the women. They each remove their tops and transition onto the bed. Spencer reaches for two pairs of handcuffs and convinces the women to chain themselves to either end of the bed. They oblige and he moves across the room and opens a closet, removing additional shackles. He uses these to bind their feet to the opposite ends of the bed from their hands. At first, they think it is foreplay, but it quickly takes a darker turn.*

*Spencer leaves for a minute before returning with a gun. He holds it to each of the women's heads in succession, causing them to scream. No one from the other rooms can hear them due to the loud party going on around the grounds of the motel. After Spencer teases the women for a minute, a knock is heard at the door.*

*Spencer motions for the women to be quiet, holding up the gun as assurance for their cooperation. He then moves to the door, opening it just a small crack to see who is disturbing them. A gruff, mustachioed man in a tan-colored, short-sleeve button down shirt and dirty jeans stares back at Spencer. "Sorry to bother you, but I'm just looking for a couple of the gals from Banjo and Sullivan? Saw them heading this way. Name's Rob. I work security for the—"*

*"Come on in, Rob, join the party!" interjects Spencer, grabbing the man's shirt and pulling him into the room in one motion. He kicks the door shut behind him and cocks the gun, aiming it square between the newcomer's eyes. "Back up."*

*Out of the corner of his eye, Rob sees the two women on the bed. They gasp, hoping that he may be able to save them. Rob raises his hands toward Spencer in concession, pleading "hold on now a minute—"*

*"Back the fuck up!" shouts Spencer, annoyance in his voice. Rob complies. "Now I want you to turn around and face that wall. I promise I won't shoot you, I just want to make sure you don't have any weapons or anything like that. Can you do that?" asks Spencer. Rob nods his head in fear before turning around and moving toward the wall. "Good. Now put your hands above your head. I'm not going to—" BANG. The gun goes off. Rob's head snaps forward and blood splatters across the wall. The women scream and flair against the handcuffs, trying to wrangle their thin wrists out from their metal prisons. "Must have slipped," adds Spencer, calmly.*

*Spencer then turns toward the women on the bed causing them to stop screaming and further tense up. "Four's a bit too crowded, huh, ladies?" he asks. "Now it's your turn," he says, looking at Gloria, the blonde.*

*"Whatever you say," says Gloria, sitting herself up slightly and nodding enthusiastically.*

*"Nah, mood's kind of ruined now," says Spencer, shaking his head. He then raises his gun and fires it into her stomach. Her bare belly thrusts downward toward the bed while her blood spurts upward and onto the ceiling. The brunette, Winnie, screams louder, then vomits in fear. A hideous mix of blood and vomit fills the air. Winnie flails around the bed, screaming and causing such a commotion that Spencer cannot keep her alive without risking someone hearing her. Just as he is about to fire the gun one last time. Otis walks into the room. Spencer and Winnie both freeze and look toward the door.*

*"Everything okay in here, Spencer?" he asks, casually. He looks around at the carnage that is in front of him before his eyes land on Winnie. She makes eye contact with him and silently pleads for her life.*

*"Yep, all set, Otis. I think you got the wrong room," replies Spencer, coolly.*

*Otis takes a deep breath, stares into the girl's eyes, then sighs. "Yeah, looks like I got the wrong room," he says, nodding. "Welp, see you later. I'll come back in and clean up in say, an hour?"*

*Spencer nods and Otis leaves. The remaining girl's body limply resigns, knowing that no one will save her. Spencer shoots her clean in the head, splattering her brains across what little white of the bedsheet can still be seen. Again he returns to the closet, this time producing a chainsaw. He pulls the cord and begins to cut the women up into small pieces. Blood splattering over the entire room. He begins to load them into two duffle bags, limb by limb, before realizing that he could probably fit these two small bodies into one bag. For what he needs, it's all right if he just mixes their parts together.*

*Spencer takes the duffle bag and loads it into the back of the Eldorado. He tears out of the parking lot as JC runs after him wondering where he is going, but to no avail. Spencer is gone, heading down I-25 South. After a couple of hours, he arrives at his destination, Truth or Consequences, New Mexico. Being the middle of the night, the streets are abandoned, giving Spencer full reign over the sleepy town. He pulls his car up to the town hall, and brings the duffle bag onto the lawn. Spencer arranges the body parts of the members of Banjo and Sullivan to form the letter "K," no one sees him, but he does it with such dexterity and stealthiness that it is clear he has done this before. He returns to his car and drives off having never encountered a soul.*

*Dawn breaks over the barren landscape and the band and crew are sleepily loading the bus for the show that day. As JC shuts the last panel to secure a large storage area at the bottom of the bus, Spencer rolls up in his Cadillac. He has the top down, seat back, and taps the side door, rallying the troops. "Look alive people," he shouts. "It's a good day to be alive!"*

*"Where have you been so early?" asks JC.*

*"Oh, just around," says Spencer enthusiastically.*

*"Well, I hope you got all your stuff out of your room. We left a real fucking mess for housekeeping, so we want to get out of here quickly."*

*"Yeah, I did a little number on my room as well. Good thing I put it in your name," jokes Spencer. JC's face falls. "I'm kidding," he adds.*

*"I just gotta go grab my stuff and we can go." Spencer steps on the gas and drives away toward his room.*

*The band plays another show, only this time, police officers flank the stage. They are onto Spencer and start to point at him. JC notices this and becomes nervous. Spencer looks at him with a glare as though he was the one who reported him. Between the second to last and last songs, Spencer approaches JC. He whispers to him so that he can be heard over the ambient noise of the crowd but so the police cannot hear him. "What did you do?"*

*"What? This guy approached me earlier," spat JC. "His name's Officer Wydell and he just had some questions. I guess his sister was in some band that was partying with us last night."*

*"What did you tell him?" asked Spencer, becoming more aggressive.*

*"Nothing, just some of the people saw you with them, I guess. I just said you'd be around after the show," JC innocently responded.*

*Spencer seethes. He channels all of his energy into the final song of the set, leaving it all on the stage. Toward the end of the song, Spencer stage dives into the pit and crowd surfs to the back of the audience. He then runs to his car and tears out of the parking lot, onto the highway. The police are still standing around. Finally, they notice Spencer has fled and make desperate calls on their radio.*

*Spencer is flying down the highway at over one-hundred miles per hour. The top is down on the vintage Eldorado. The wind is in his hair and his leather jacket flaps behind him. Ahead, a row of police officers stand ready to block Spencer from continuing down the road; he is facing sure death. He pulls out a shotgun and stands up over the windshield. Suddenly, within his own dream, the doctor appears. He is standing between the police and Spencer. Just as the moment of impact arrives, when Spencer will crash into the doctor, they all disappear into the ether.*

Doctor Black woke up. It was morning and he had barely gotten any rest, spending much of the night tossing and turning while his mind danced with visions of murder. He began to make notes of his dreams, just in case they matched anything Spencer would say in the future. He knew that what he saw in his dreams could not be real. For one thing, he distinctly remembered JC being in the dream, but he had disappeared months before this recent tour, so would certainly have not been present. He was most concerned about the visions he saw of himself, metaphorically saving Spencer from the police. He again questioned if protecting Spencer and his potential culpability for his crimes was the right thing to do.

Later that morning, Wendy drove Doctor Black to the airport herself; they barely spoke on the ride. She worried for her brother, and he could tell. He appreciated getting to spend the time with her, but now it was back to his life, back to his patients. He would be seeing Spencer that next Monday, as soon as they had both returned from across the country. He hugged his sister goodbye and exchanged the usual pleasantries. Less than four hours after leaving the inn, he was in the air high over the Rocky Mountains and heading due east. He landed back at Boston Logan Airport later that night and went straight to bed. The following weekend passed by with uneventful monotony as he approached his first day back to work that Monday.

Monday had him seeing a shorter list of patients than usual. Each commented to the doctor that they were excited to get back to their sessions and had missed him during the unannounced break. Some had seen Nancy, but others had just taken the last few weeks off from their therapy. Spencer would be his last patient of the day, as usual, and the doctor's excitement to hear what he had gotten up to made it difficult to listen to any of the patients that he saw beforehand.

For the first time in his history of meeting with Doctor Black, Spencer arrived early for his appointment. He had been back from his recent tour for a day or two and felt like for, at least these few days, he was rushing around a lot less than usual; he had some well-deserved relaxation time. Doctor Black stood up and greeted Spencer in his usual awkward manner. The two then took their seats, Spencer plopping down onto the couch and the doctor returning to his office chair. He had wheeled it out from behind his desk and now adjusted it a few more inches so that he could better face his patient.

As the session continued, the doctor had hoped to hear about the killing spree, even if inadvertently, through Spencer's dreams. His own dream had plagued him and he yearned to hear if Spencer had one that was similar. Sadly, he was let down. His weekend of anticipation ended in disappointment, as Spencer recounted only what seemed to be a particularly successful yet uneventful tour. No strange nightmares, just the open road and the loving fans. It once again forced the doctor to question his private accusations of Spencer and whether or not he was reading too much into these dreams, much like he had read too much into his nephew, Tony, and the dead rabbits.

# X
# The World in My Hands

Doctor Ian Black was not his usual, jovial self. In fact, he realized that he had not been this version of himself for some months. Truly, if he could trace the onset of these morose feelings, it would be around the end of the summer—around the time when he first met Spencer, and when his rival, Colin Barlow, had been on the cover of that dreadful magazine, *Psychiatry Now*. From that moment until the present one, he had been in some kind of a funk. Now, here he was, sitting in his office, alone and reflecting. The clock above the desk ticked away, it's secondhand slowly counting down the last fractions of the workday. With the office being closed through the new year, he had just about an hour until his last appointment of 2018, an appointment which would be with Spencer. This would be the final session in another wasted year, as the doctor had little to show for his trip around the sun.

Sitting in his office chair, Doctor Black thought about how he had gone another 365 days being unpublished, unaccomplished, and unexcited about anything for his future. He had hit a dead-end on his book after finally accepting that Spencer was not the psychotic killer that he hoped he was and had returned from his sister's place a broken man. Lost. Alone. Unable to listen to his patient's thoughts or needs. His outer wounds from the bar, the scrapes and cuts, had healed, but it was the deeper cuts of the inner-psyche that now ravaged him. He was in need of a friend, an ally. *Maybe he should try across the hall,* he thought to himself. He might just be able to catch Nancy before she went home for the day. Maybe she could shed some light on the darkness that he felt within.

Doctor Black walked into Nancy's office to find her back toward him in a tight-fitting navy blue dress. He took a moment to admire the way it formed around her perfect ass, gaining a closer look as he took a step into the office. Startled at his footsteps, Nancy abruptly turned around and held up the scissors she had in her hand, causing him to back a step and let out a small yelp while putting his hands up.

"Sorry!" she said. "You scared me. I was just wrapping some gifts." She lowered the scissors. Behind her a small brown box sat amidst a flurry of red, green, and white wrapping paper.

"Not at all. Sorry to bother you," he replied. "I just wondered if we might be able to chat for a few moments."

"Sure, I've got some time. I wasn't going to leave for another thirty minutes or so. I'm ducking out a bit early today for a hair appointment."

"Excellent. Yes. Well..." said the doctor, plopping himself down uninvited into one of the comfy large patient chairs that sat in front of her desk. Noting that this encounter might take a while, Nancy sighed and moved the half-wrapped present onto a laptop and stack of files that sat toward the edge of her desk. She then moved behind the desk and slipped into her office chair.

"So. What's going on?" she asked, leaning back and comfortably assuming the role of the psychiatrist.

"Well. Uh," he began slowly, unsure of whether or not he could phrase his emotions and thoughts exactly as he was feeling them. "This is rather a good deal harder on this side of things isn't it? I just mean, normally we've got it easy, being the ones to listen and not have to sift through our inner workings."

"I never thought of it as easy. But I certainly see what you mean," Nancy retorted.

"Yes, of course. So, it's just…lately, I've been feeling a sort of…" he searched for the word and then it came. "Imposter syndrome, you might call it. It's rather as if my whole career has been for nothing. That I've reached a point where I haven't earned anything for myself or built anything of my own. At the same time, I dole out advice to others as though I have the answers. As if my opinion matters."

"When do you suppose this started?"

"It would have to be a few months back," he replied. "Probably starting with Colin Barlow being on that magazine cover. I'm sure I've mentioned him before. And I haven't been sleeping well…the occasional odd dream. Then, I had some issues with a misunderstanding regarding a patient."

"You didn't do anything illegal, I hope!" she interjected.

"No, no. Of course not. I just found myself making assumptions that one of my patients was something that he wasn't. That's all. I only did it to further my career and to write this bloody book, which really isn't going anywhere anyways. But now I am starting to believe my original assumption about this patient was actually correct, yet I have no evidence."

"So it is criminal?"

"Well, yes, on the patient's part. If it's at all true," replied the doctor, beginning to speak faster as his thoughts spiraled out of control. "Which it may well not be. This entire situation has had me questioning everything. I started routinely asking myself 'how did I end up here?' I just feel so lost and on my own, in search of something real. But when I think I've found it, it turns out to be a fabrication. An invention. Does that make sense?"

"Yeah. But, wow. I had no idea, Ian" she consoled. "You know, it's not uncommon to feel this way around the holidays. I don't have to tell you this, I'm sure you know already, but it can be a lonely time for a lot of people. Especially those without someone to share it with."

"It's true," said Doctor Black. He leaned back in the chair contemplating for a moment what she had said. There had to be something more than just seasonal depression and loneliness. He sighed then added. "But the thing about it is, I was just visiting with my sister and seeing how well she and her husband are doing made me almost feel worse. Sometimes it feels easier to withdraw from the world."

"That can be true, too. End of the year? Taking stock of your life? It's very common, Ian. A lot of patients present with this." She looked down to the drawer on her left and opened it up. "Here," she said, producing a small unlabeled pill bottle. "I have some samples for this. A drug rep dropped it off. It should help you out a bit. Just to help you sleep and maybe feel a little better for a few days. Completely non-habit forming, so you can take them for a few days then stop. No problem."

Doctor Black looked at the bottle for a moment. Usually he was not one to look to medication for the answers. It went again almost all of his training, but here was Nancy, trying to help, and he should at least acknowledge the gesture. "Thank you. I'll give it a whirl," he said, taking the bottle and slipping it into the pocket of his dress slacks.

"You're worth more than you're giving yourself credit for, you know? And for what it's worth, I feel lonely sometimes too. I don't talk about it much, but I obviously had to sacrifice some things for my career at every step of the way. And you don't see it in the moment, but looking back? That's when it becomes clearer, hindsight being what it is. I've actually been working on the other aspects of my life for a while now and I've even recently started seeing someone."

"Oh. That's....wonderful," he said, gritting his teeth and forcing himself to smile to not let on the slightest bit of jealousy at whoever this person might be. It's not that he felt he had any chance at a relationship with Nancy, it was just that he did not like the fact that someone else might. It further left a sickening taste in his mouth to think of someone else being happy, even Nancy, in this moment when he was so miserable.

"It's a former patient, so I can't really talk about it. It's not unethical or anything. Former patient that I only saw one time. I also discussed it with the local ethics board, so—"

"You talked to Tony about it?" Doctor Black interjected.

"Doctor Lovato?" she asked rhetorically. "Yeah, he said it sounded fine to him. Kim Boggs too, when I asked her. I didn't know you were on a first-name basis with Tony Lovato."

"Oh, no. I'm not, really. I just..." he stammered, nervous that he had been outed for a feigned connection to someone he had met just one time and under difficult circumstances.

"I know you've had your issues with the board after they threatened your license, but it's nice to see you've smoothed it over," she said smiling. "See? Things aren't going that badly. It's all a frame of mind. But I do need to get going, so..." she gestured toward the present on her desk. "If I can get back to this and then head out?"

"Yes, of course," stuttered the doctor, awkwardly getting up out of the chair. "I've got a patient in a few moments myself. So not a bother."

"Oh yes, that's right," she remembered.

"What is?" he asked.

"That you have a patient," she said slowly. He stared at her quizzically. She paused for a moment as her eyes widened, before adding, "I think you said so when you came in."

"Ah, yes. Of course. Well I'm off. Ta-ta for now," the doctor laughed.

Making his way across the hall was quick work as Karen had been given off for the holidays and was, therefore, not present to torment him with some task needing doing or some payment he was late on. He left the door to his office open, given that there was no replacement receptionist in the waiting area, then found his way back into his desk chair. Once there, he took a moment to himself, checking the clock and realizing that Spencer was due any minute. As soon as he had straightened the magazines on the coffee table and cleaned up some empty coffee cups strewn around his desk, he heard a knock from the open door.

"Hey, Doc, how are ya?" said Spencer from the door frame. "All right if I come in?"

"Sure, sure. Make yourself right at home!" said Doctor Black.

The session went as they all typically did. Spencer was back to sharing his disturbing dreams while also discussing some aspects of his life. The difference, however, was that Doctor Black found himself unable to concentrate. He was listening intently, but only for some clue, some hint that Spencer might not be who he said he was. His notes were sparse and scattered at best, choosing only key moments to focus on. At one point he thought to himself that he could no longer be an effective therapist to this patient if he did not come out with some form of apology and explain himself. Just as he thought he had his chance to interject, Spencer came to an interesting part of his dream, and the doctor once again found his interest piqued.

"I'm standing below two bodies as they hang in front of me," said Spencer. "And as I see my reflection in the mirror, behind the bodies, I see my face painted white. Like some sort of a clown, or a mime. But now it's my turn to laugh. And then I wake up."

This sounded like it might be a thinly veiled cover, an admission that Spencer was the man behind the bar. This dream seemed to be the closest Spencer came to describing real-life events that the doctor could corroborate; he had seen the two bodies on the news, and had most likely been beaten up by the men earlier that same night. While he did not know the circumstances of the teen suicides, or the mass murder at the camp, it followed that the other dreams could be real as well. He was half listening and half remembering things that Spencer had said before, unable to focus completely on what he was telling him in the present moment. Realizing that his thoughts were drifting, he once again began to think of the words that he needed to say, the words he would use to end his relationship with this patient; he was, after all, unable to help him and only hurting himself the longer he kept this relationship.

As Spencer recounted his plans for the upcoming holidays including a visit to New York to see family and a charity event for children where he would be dressed as Santa, the doctor felt the pain in his side creep up as he became more stressed over what he next needed to do. After hearing about the plans of Spencer's drive to and from New York, the doctor finally interrupted him. "It's wonderful that you'll be driving down to visit family, Spencer. And doing some charity work at the same time. I wondered, though, if I might say something for a moment here, seeing as we're almost out of time."

"Of course. The hour really flew by, huh?"

"Yes, as it tends to do," the doctor replied. "So, I know that I apologized at the hospital and I'm still not quite certain what happened that night. I'm not sure that I can be your therapist anymore, going forward." As soon as he said the words he regretted them; he would be losing his most famous patient, as well as the potential serial killer for his book. He was unable to shake this thought no matter how implausible it was becoming.

"Wow," said Spencer. He was stunned. He took it in for a moment before continuing. "I had no idea you felt that way. I was hoping maybe we had buried the hatchet. So to speak. But, this. This sort of came out of nowhere."

"Yes, I imagine it did. Although, I have been thinking about it for some time. But, perhaps…maybe I'm being too abrupt," the doctor replied, changing his tone. "I wonder if you could take a couple of weeks, over the holidays, and write down exactly what it is you're seeking to do with therapy? What goals you have. Maybe then we can discuss it and see if that's something that I can help you with, or if I'm only getting in the way. I wouldn't want to hinder your recovery with any…" he searched for the correct word. "…hang-ups that I might have."

Spencer paused a moment, then continued, smiling, "Ah, now I see. I'm onto you."

"How's that?" asked the doctor, his interest piqued.

"You're trying to push the therapy along with all that 'not wanting to be my therapist' stuff. I got ya. Thank you. I will definitely get right on that."

"You're very quick," the doctor admired, realizing that he perhaps had an opportunity to take back his words. "That's good. That will help as we move forward, as will the goals. I was also hoping to have a more complete picture of everything from your previous therapist, Doctor Michaelson, but we still haven't heard from his office, although Karen seems to have contacted a former employee of his and will hopefully straighten it out when she gets back."

"That's great news," replied Spencer, slightly dejected at all that had occurred. "I guess I have some work to do myself while we're off. Some self-reflection."

"Yes, and thank you again for agreeing to do it."

Spencer got up from the chair. He picked up his water bottle, tucked it into the back pocket of his slim-fit black jeans and put back on his leather jacket. "See you in a couple weeks," he said as he headed toward the door.

"See you," replied the doctor. He waited until Spencer was out of the building before he hurried to his desk and pulled out a Dictaphone tape recorder. He spoke into it, remarking, "Notes from session December twenty-first, twenty-eighteen. Spencer appeared surprised when told that I could not be his therapist. Perhaps he is capable of emotions after all. However, subject will be traveling to New York, note to self: keep an eye out for any news reports from that area over the holidays."

The doctor clicked the "stop" button on the recorder and slipped it into his jacket pocket. Done for the day, he began to pack up his belongings. He noticed the Christmas card from his other sister, Linnea, on his desk. Here she was with her insufferable husband and those horrible beasts she called children, smiling wider than should be allowed by law. Despite feeling particularly grinchy for that one moment, he thought it might cheer him up a bit to at least see some family for the upcoming holiday. He was going to accept her invitation after all, knowing full well that he could leave at any time, as she lived just across town. On his way out of the building, he noticed Nancy's office light was no longer on; she had left. He was all alone. Despite what Nancy had said to him earlier, he relished being by himself. For a few moments before hitting traffic, noise, and commotion in the outside world, he sat in the office, enjoying the silence of the night.

# XI
## Merry Axe-mas

Linnea Chapman's house was decorated with its yearly Christmas-enhanced suburban-splendor with white lights illuminating the large, red brick Georgian home, and the white shutters flanking candle-filled windows. The lush green shrubbery surrounding the house was further adorned with lights and the yard held tastefully placed seasonal statues, not the tacky inflatables some of the neighbors had on their lawns. Linnea certainly had an eye for design, and with the money her husband, Bill, earned, she also had the time and means to keep it.

As he approached the door, toting a few measly gift bags thoughtlessly filled with gift cards, the doctor felt a feeling of dread wash over him. *Why had he agreed to come here for Christmas*, he thought. If there was one place he was certain to feel worse about his own station in life, it was at his perfect sister's perfect house during a major holiday that afforded her every opportunity to entertain and show off. Like a mouse wandering into a cheese-laid trap, the enticement of an excellent meal would not be without consequence for the doctor; he could feel it chill him to his spine, the hairs on his back standing as he shuddered at the thought of what would greet him on the other side of the door. He rang the bell, regretting it almost as soon as he had.

Inside, a dog barked and children yelled jubilantly. Linnea's oldest, Bill Jr., or Billy, was fourteen; then there was Richard, Ricky as they called him, who was eleven; and the youngest, Laura, was eight. As the door opened the glow of the warm hallway light spilled out onto the brick steps the doctor stood on. He was immediately greeted by the five smiling faces of his sister and her family.

The house was gigantic—something straight out of a John Hughes movie—and perfect for Christmas. Straight ahead from the hallway was a path that led to the kitchen, as well as stairs leading to the bedrooms on the next floor. In the living room to his left, the doctor could see the beautifully decorated Christmas tree that must have been ten feet high but still did not touch the ceiling. Across from the tree, a fire roared in the fireplace, casting its flickering red light across the room. To the right of the hallway was a formal dining room that held a chandelier hanging above a cherry wood table that was perfectly-set for six.

Doctor Black's coat was taken by Billy, the eldest, and Laura took his bags and placed them beneath their behemoth of a tree. The usual pleasantries were exchanged and he was offered a drink, which he declined at first, but decided one couldn't hurt and it was the holidays. He resigned himself to stick to only one this time, as he had taken some of the medication given to him by his colleague, Doctor Nancy Price, if the need should arise. He reasoned that the need most certainly would have arisen if he stayed here in Pleasantville for too long. Not only was the family disgustingly perfect, but Bill Sr. had the tendency to mock Doctor Black's profession and the very foundation of psychology in general. They differed on everything from politics, which Bill cared nothing for but still spouted his ill-informed opinions, to sports, which the doctor cared nothing for, but nevertheless made vain attempts to discuss then and always sounded stupid. Tonight would certainly not be the exception, as he knew that when Bill got a little liquor in him, he was off to the races. Linnea was the youngest, and thus spent more of her youth in America rather than in England, like the doctor and Wendy had. The doctor assumed that this nurturing must have contributed to her bad-taste in brutish men.

"Why don't you go down to see Bill's man-cave, as he calls it?" offered Linnea. "He has a bar down there and can fix you a drink while you talk about man stuff. Won't that be nice, Ian? I'll bring down some little app-ies as soon as I have them ready!"

"Lovely," responded the doctor, a saccharine tone in an attempt to go along to get along.

"Sounds great!" hollered Bill, an overly enthusiastic response that was coupled with an unnecessarily strong clap on the back, pushing Doctor Black forward with its force. "I love showing off this little man cave I've got. This one's for the boys!" he shouted with an overly masculine tone. "Am I right, Ian?"

"Absolutely. I'd love to see it," managing to sound even less manly than usual.

"Boys," said Bill, addressing his sons. "Why don't you come on down too, show Uncle Ian our little home within the home?" He then turned back to Ian saying, "They've got some video games and stuff down there, it's good for them to get the energy and aggression out a bit away from the rest of the house, you know? Or I guess not, you never had kids. But if you do, take my advice on this one." Bill always managed to make a dig at the doctor, even when he was trying to be nice.

They descended into the basement, where Doctor Black was instantly confronted with an overload of sports memorabilia and an impressively built bar area. A beige carpet and surrounding wood paneling gave the room a brighter and larger feel than he had anticipated. As the centerpiece of the room, a large television was affixed to the wall opposite the stairs. Facing the television were two dark-green leather couches that had a mess of wires and video game systems in front of them. The doctor strolled over to the bar, admiring the work and care that must have gone into building the walnut wood bar top. Just as impressive, the selection of alcohols rivaled that of a restaurant. Bill had even managed to illuminate the glass shelves from below, highlighting some of the more expensive bottles as they spanned across the back of the bar.

"Can I get you something?" said Bill. "Pretty good selection, huh?" He knew that it was but wanted to hear Ian say it.

"Yes. Very. Um, maybe just a small glass of that whiskey there. The Irish one. On the end."

"Ah, the O'Brien Twelve-Year. Good stuff. My father's favorite too."

"I'll try that one then," said the doctor. He picked up the top glass from a neatly stacked tower at the end of the bar. "Just a small one please."

Bill poured out the whiskey as the boys started playing with their video games. Doctor Black turned around at the sound of shots fired, eventually realizing that it was just the high volume of the game coming from the television. As he turned back to Bill, embarrassed at his jumpiness, he noticed a large set of deer antlers mounted to the wall. "Nice rack," said the doctor, laughing to himself at his joke.

Bill paused for a moment. "Huh, good one," he replied, impressed that his brother-in-law was capable of a joke. "Shot that myself. I don't really get out hunting anymore but used to love it. Your sister isn't too fond of that thing. Or hunting at all, really."

A few minutes later Linnea called down to the boys to come up and get ready for dinner. The doctor and Bill followed. On the way up the stairs, Bill stopped Doctor Black. "Hey, Ian. You all right? You seem particularly on edge today?"

"Do I?" replied the doctor, feigned astonishment on his face, as he knew something was wrong and that he was just unable to disguise it.

"Yeah, could be just me. You just seem…angry. Usually you're so happy, it's annoying," joked Bill. "I don't know. I'm just trying to be brotherly. Truth be told, Linnea was the one who wanted to know. She asked me to check after she heard something from Wendy."

"Oh. Well, that's very nice of you," replied the doctor. "Maybe I have been a little down, but it's nice to be with family. Thanks again for inviting me. I'll try not to be annoyingly sad or annoyingly happy. Maybe just…annoyingly neutral shall we say?"

"Whatever you say. Like I said, Linnea was concerned. Maybe just make her feel good and pretend a bit. For my sake? And hers."

The doctor said nothing, acknowledging Bill with a simple look and a nod just as he reached the top of the stairs and proceeded into the main hallway. In the dining room, his sister's smiling face greeted him from behind a large turkey that she was just setting down on the table to carve. It was picturesque. How could her life be going so perfectly, when his was, simply put, not.

The dinner was incredible. Turkey with all of its usual fixings and side dishes, including buttery mashed potatoes, two types of savory stuffing, a perfect gravy, and root vegetables. Wine was poured and the doctor had a glass each of red and white. The meal was finished in the fashion of tradition with an excellently layered trifle for dessert, just as Linnea and Ian's mother used to make for them in their youth. Immediately thereafter, they moved on to another British tradition, popping their Christmas crackers, which sent small waves of confetti into the air and produced pieces of paper and trinkets from the inside of the cardboard tubes. As Doctor Black sat around looking at this perfect family donning the paper crowns that had come out of the crackers, his face beamed a smile. For a minute, he felt good, and the pain in his gut had disappeared.

A few moments later, as Linnea and Bill were cleaning up, Billy, Ricky, and Laura got up from the table and ran into the other room to play with some of their newly-acquired Christmas toys. The doctor once again found himself alone with only his thoughts as his companions. After a moment of reflection, he came to a realization: his sister's family had let him into their lives and their hearts, and he hoped he would find the same joy and love for himself someday. From underneath his ill-fitting red paper crown, he started to get choked up, a tear forming in the corner of his eye. Having just started to wipe away the collecting bead of water, the doctor was joined by his sister, who returned to the room to continue clearing the plates and settings. He quickly wiped his eyes, blamed his allergies, and attempted to regain his masculinity. She, however, seeing sadness in her brother, sat down with him, reaching out and taking his hand as she did. Their eyes met and she gave him a knowing smile that only a sister could.

A flood of thoughts and emotions rushed into the doctor's mind. He was relearning the meaning of Christmas, that joy and love are more important than fame and fortune. In this moment, he vowed that it would bring him some solace in the new year that was soon to come. He would take Nancy's prescribed medicine and begin to work on himself from within, healing as though he were both patient and doctor. He would become his most important client, and focus on self-care. He realized that, in a way, he had Spencer to thank for this. Had he not misjudged this individual so egregiously—not lost his mind while trying to create facts where only fiction lived—he might never have ascertained that he was unhappy and needed to make some changes to his life.

The moment between Doctor black and his sister, Linnea, was interrupted by the sounds of a television loudly emanating across the hall from the living room. Linnea yelled into the next room, asking her children to turn down the volume. When the request went unanswered, she and the doctor started toward the noise. Upon entering, they found Billy, standing in front of the television that was affixed to the wall above the fireplace. The TV displayed a news report of a brutal murder that happened earlier that day, one state away, in East Proctor, Connecticut.

"Oh my god," gasped Linnea. "What is this you're watching?"

"It's insane, Mom," replied Billy "Some crazy guy in a Santa suit killed these people."

"Turn that trash off," snapped Linnea. "You don't need to scare your brother and sister."

"Wait just a tick, Lin," interjected the doctor. "I'm curious to hear this. Maybe just for a minute? Billy, can you just turn it down a bit, perhaps? That way we don't disturb the others."

"Sure, Uncle Ian."

Linnea scoffed at her brother but ultimately gave in. They watched together for a few moments as their image of a perfect Christmas was shattered. The newscasters reported that a madman dressed like Santa Claus had been spotted fleeing the scene of a crime. They had no suspects and eyewitness testimony was sketchy at best, but the murderer had committed a severe massacre. Along the side of a country road, a married couple had been butchered in the blistering cold while their son looked on, and eventually, was left alive. The son had been taken into police custody until he could be released to a surviving family member.

The newscast immediately reminded the doctor of Spencer's dream about the young boy who was the lone survivor from an attack on his babysitter and her friends. It all felt so familiar and yet far away.

Linnea gasped at the news, while his nephew, Billy, remained silent, shocked from what he was witnessing. Doctor Black imagined that for Billy it was like learning that Santa Claus was not real all over again. Only in this case Santa Claus was real, and he was a murderer. The thought briefly entered the mind of the doctor that Spencer was in the Connecticut area. He could not help himself, as he knew for sure that Spencer had gone to visit family in New York for the holidays but not where he currently was. Surely he would have driven through Connecticut at some point in either direction. He had to stop himself from this line of thinking, as he remembered that it had never gotten him anywhere but miserable, so he soon dismissed it as merely a coincidence. Spencer had done an appearance dressed as Santa Claus the night before and was most likely still in New York. The doctor silently scolded himself for obsessing over this one patient and trying to hold onto something that could simply not be proven with real data or facts.

After a few minutes of news coverage, the report ended and a new story began. Linnea turned the television off, deciding to look away from the evils of the world and return to a day full of joyful mirth. She suggested that the children and Ian open their presents for each other there in the living room and called for the rest of the family.

While waiting for the others to join, the doctor once again returned to his thoughts of Spencer. It was strange to see reports of yet another mysterious murder that turned up no suspects and occurred in a location that Spencer was traveling to. If Spencer were a serial killer who traveled from place to place to avoid getting caught, being a musician would be the perfect cover. Of course, he still lacked evidence, and Spencer had likely been the man who saved his life behind the bar, hardly the modus operandi of a serial killer.

Doctor Black remained distant from his sister and her family for the rest of the evening. The painful feeling of dread in the pit of his stomach increased, causing him to excuse himself shortly after the exchanging of gifts. He had stayed his welcome and his family hardly noticed or missed his presence. Bill Sr. had passed out on the couch in the basement watching a football game and the children were preoccupied with their new toys. The only person he had really enjoyed seeing, Linnea, was so exhausted from having put together another perfect Christmas that she was past the point of fun, although she kept this exhaustion to herself, never letting others see her pain or hard work. In some ways, the doctor envied her; in others, she envied him. He had always wanted to find someone to settle down with like Linnea had, but he had spent so much of his life solely focused on his career that there was little time to do so. His colleague Nancy had done much the same and he always wondered if maybe the two of them might work out, but she was still young and so beautiful, and he was quite the opposite. She was also newly taken, he had just learned. As for Linnea, she envied her brother while she wished that she had a career of her own, something that she had built herself outside of the home. She loved her husband and children very much but dreamt about all of the undiscovered wonders of the world that existed beyond the walls of her perfect house. Ian had returned to England for a few years to attend Oxford and now had an interesting career dealing with the minds of the disturbed. Wendy had moved to rural Colorado to experience the expansiveness of the West. Linnea, however, had stayed put in their small New England town. This lack of mobility often made her feel small and insignificant, especially when looking at the lives of her siblings.

The brother and sister let their mutual feelings of envy go undiscussed and parted ways, promising to see each other soon but knowing that it may be months before they would reunite despite their close proximity. Doctor Black walked down the brick steps and across the beautifully manicured lawn—even in winter it was perfect, with a light dusting of snow. He approached his small car and got in. The pain in his side was increasing with each minute that his feeling of unease remained. Sitting in the driver's seat, he reached over to the glove compartment, where he had kept the pills that Nancy gave him, and removed the bottle. He popped one into his mouth and was struck with a memory about one of the last times that he was in his car.

Since the night at the bar, the doctor had not been driving much, having been first hospitalized and then away visiting Wendy. Between those two events, he had to get his car out of the impound, where it was towed for having been left on the street while he was in the hospital. One of his last memories that driving evoked for him was that of Spencer leaning into his window and turning off the stereo that was playing their sessions aloud. Knowing that Spencer's building was not too out of the way of his journey home, he thought he might drive by. If Spencer's car was out front, or his lights were on and he was home, the doctor would know that he came home, and thus, may have come through Connecticut at just the right time. Of course, if his car was not there it would not prove Spencer's innocence but rather would give the doctor some sense of comfort that he could use to stop obsessing over this single patient's actions. He put the bottle of pills back into his glove compartment and started driving toward Spencer's house.

# XII
## Love Bites

Doctor Black drove twice around the lot that stood behind Spencer's building, searching for his patient's parking space. Piles of brown, dirt-stained snow ringed the lot, remnants of a storm from a few nights prior. Cars were sprinkled throughout the asphalt lot, some with snow still dusted over them, undriven for multiple days. There were two bright street lamps illuminating the lot, as well as the light of the full moon, but the doctor still had difficulty finding what he was looking for. On one occasion he had to get out of his vehicle to read the space numbers marked on the pavement, the biting chill of the night air forcing him quickly back inside. He was searching for the marker that correlated with Spencer's unit number, sixteen, the penthouse. Finally, from inside his car, he found what he needed. There were two spaces allocated to Spencer, to be exact; two adjacent spots next to the lot's rear entrance that exited onto a side street behind the building. One of Spencer's spaces was empty, the other held a small red car that looked familiar to the doctor but which was covered in snow. Neither space held Spencer's car, leading the doctor to the conclusion that he may still be in New York.

The doctor pulled his own vehicle into an open spot against the building in order to get out and have a closer look at this mysterious second vehicle. It could have belonged to a neighbor or a friend, he reasoned. It could also have been another car belonging to Spencer. Either way, he needed to brush off the snow and see if he could garner anything from its presence in Spencer's space. No sooner had he touched the handle of his own car door to get out when a car came screaming into the lot from the front entrance. The lights danced across his face as they turned around the row of cars that he sat in. Finally, the new arrival barreled right into Spencer's vacant spot. The doctor tensed up, his hair standing on end, fearing he would be caught spying for a second time. His car was switched off and he remained in the shadow of the building, not illuminated by the street lamps that were scattered around the lot. Here he would hopefully be safe, but any movement might tip off Spencer or whomever had just pulled into his parking space.

The doctor quickly found out that it was Spencer himself. He watched him as he got out of his car, wearing a black, hooded sweatshirt with a five-pointed star, a pentagram, emblazoned on the front. With Spencer arriving home in this moment, it meant that he would have passed through East Proctor, Connecticut, at just the right time to murder that entire family. The doctor's blood pulsed, his mind raced. While he was missing any shred of proof that Spencer had done these horrible deeds, the possibility was enough for the doctor to become concerned. He was increasingly unable to chalk these happenings up as being mere coincidences. Another thought occurred to him: if it was Spencer that killed that family, it might be worth studying this moment. He had never seen a patient this close in time to an actual killing. In all of his years of work, the patients that he studied had mostly been incarcerated, usually for years after their last crime. He knew that this timeframe could be dangerous. Spencer always seemed calm and collected during their sessions, but those would have been days, if not weeks, after the murders had been committed. While this heightened the reward for the research, it also heightened the danger; if Spencer had caught him now, he might still be in a rage state, endangering the doctor.

While some in the field believed that a "rage state" theory was often only exploited by defendants attempting to blame their emotions for their actions, the doctor understood that during the actual committing of a murder, the chemistry inside a killers brain was transformed. Little was known in this area, primarily due to the ethical questions, and practical availability, regarding the use of functional magnetic resonance imaging (fMRI) during an actual killing. If possible, which it surely was not, this would register and report the changes that were happening within the brain during such a time. Given that there was some disagreement in the field over whether or not a killer might be more inclined to kill again following an initial murder, the doctor had always wanted to find this answer; he may have be able to stake his career on it. However, when the next life taken could potentially be his own, his desire to discover the answer suddenly slipped away. He became nervous that, if Spencer saw him now, he may become the most recent victim in what could potentially be an ever-elongating string of crimes. That is, of course, if he did it at all.

The doctor watched as Spencer moved toward the rear of his car, opened the backseat door on the driver's side, and seconds later produced a brown leather duffle bag, which he promptly popped up on top of the trunk. From his vantage point, the doctor had a perfect view of the bag and was able to see the fluffy sleeve of a red and white Santa coat sticking out from the zipper. He knew Spencer had been in New York doing charity work, but these coincidences seemed farther fetched than could be possible. It was a case of Occam's Razor; the simplest solution is most likely the correct solution, which, in this case, suggested that Spencer was, in fact, a murderer. Doctor Black may not have discovered the smoking gun, the one piece of evidence that would show Spencer for what he truly was, but he was in hot pursuit. Perhaps if he could get his hands on that duffle bag, or maybe some DNA from the car. He would quickly bring it to the authorities, and he would then be able to write his book all about how he had discovered and studied this real-life killer. Being that he would be the first to learn about it, he would become the definitive source on the serial killer's brain as he, or she, stalked their victims. He again started to feel giddy. Spencer was going to make his career.

Spencer next walked around to the passenger side door, which gave the doctor a look at the back of the sweatshirt that had the words "Slaughtered Lamb" written across it. This did little to lower the doctor's fear in the moment, wondering if Spencer was, after all, a wolf in sheep's clothing, or if perhaps Doctor Black himself was the sheep, ready for the slaughter.

Spencer opened the door revealing a companion. Until now, the doctor had not realized that Spencer had someone with him. From his vantage point, Doctor Black could only see that she wore a tight black dress under a red coat that matched the car in the adjacent space. Perhaps it was this woman's car. Her face was obscured by Spencer, then she turned away and retrieved some luggage from the passenger side back seat. Spencer pulled this woman in for a kiss and spun her around. The woman's highlighted brown hair first caught the moonlight as she twirled, then caught Spencer's hand as he caressed the back of her head. Their lips lingered over one another as they slowly pulled away from a long, passionate kiss.

Doctor Black felt the pain in his gut just a split second before his brain registered what his eyes were looking at. There in the parking lot, kissing Spencer, was Doctor Nancy Price. It was a betrayal that he could not have seen coming. Spencer was a charming fellow, the doctor knew, but he could potentially be dangerous. After the initial shock of the moment wore off, the doctor became increasingly nervous. Nancy could be in peril, and he could potentially need to be the one to save her. Even if Spencer was not a serial killer, he was certainly a disturbed patient, but she had no idea. As far as Nancy knew, Spencer was a nice chap with some bad dreams, he reasoned. Perhaps he should have shared more with her, but he never in a million years thought that she would develop a relationship with a patient, let alone this particular one. She had told him that she was seeing a former patient, and now it all made sense as to why she was not more forthcoming.

Spencer and Nancy loaded her luggage into the red car; the doctor now understood why it had seemed so familiar to him. At this point, he had seen enough. He turned the keys in the ignition and started his car. In the same movement as he turned over the ignition, he flipped on his high beams, causing both Spencer and Nancy to look toward him before shielding their eyes at the brightness of the lights. They shrugged, thinking little of the car leaving the lot, and returned to a parting kiss. Doctor Black sped the car away and out through the front entrance of the building's parking lot.

The doctor sped down the streets of Salem, toward his home, the wheels in his mind outpacing the wheels on his car. He had turned into a madman almost instantly, wracked with questions about Spencer and Nancy and their relationship. It was as if this new knowledge had transformed him and he would never be the same, doomed to have it eat away at him from the inside out for the rest of the time he walked the earth; it was instantly tearing him apart. How had he not seen this? How could he miss it? His brain was so consumed with the two lovers that he almost missed his phone vibrating from the cupholder between the two front seats. The buzzing finally snapped him out of his trance and he picked up his phone to check the caller ID. It was Karen. He wondered what she could possibly want on Christmas night but nevertheless answered the phone.

"Hello?" asked the doctor.

"There you are. I called you four times!" Karen said, her voice annoyed.

"Karen? Sorry, I must have missed it. I was a bit preoccupied," the doctor responded sheepishly.

"You told me to call you as soon as I had the files for Spencer from Doctor Michaelson's office? Well, I got them," she said, proud that she was finally doing something right for a change.

"You did?" the doctor asked, unenthusiastically. "I'm not sure I can really face them right now…uh, Christmas and all, you know?"

"I think you will want to take a look at these. Are you out right now? Any chance you can pick them up? Trust me." said Karen, stone-voiced and adamant.

The doctor sighed before acquiescing, "Sure, what's your address?"

"81 Landis Road. It's off Yorkshire. See you soon."

Doctor Black hung up the phone and punched her address into his GPS. On the way he felt the pain in his stomach increase. Maybe he needed to up the dosage on the meds he had gotten from Nancy.

He arrived at Karen's just a few minutes later, as it was approximately equidistant between Spencer's house and the office, which was on his way home. He pulled up to the front of her triple-decker, wood-framed building and waited a moment for Karen to come outside. While waiting, he reached into the glove compartment and took another pill from the bottle, swallowing it down dry. Karen came outside almost immediately after, sauntering toward his car. She had a red hooded sweatshirt pulled up over her curly hair and sweatpants, not the usual office attire that the doctor was accustomed to seeing her wear. For footwear, she sported a pair of brown flip flops, her feet exposed to the elements. She approached the car and he rolled the window down for her on the passenger side.

"Get in. You must be freezing out there," shouted the doctor, noticing her feet as she ran toward him.

"Thanks," said Karen, taking him up on his offer and entering the vehicle.

"So. Where are the files?" he snapped, impatient and ready to get home.

"Here," glowered Karen, handing over a thumb drive to the doctor. "They're on here. It's a bunch of session videos. And from what I saw, it's really not good."

"You watched them?!" he spat. "These are privileged conversations between a doctor and his patient. You can't go watching these things."

"After Chelsea showed up unannounced—"

"Who?"

"Chelsea. Talmadge? I think that's her name. She's Doctor Michaelson's assistant. Well, former assistant," said Karen. "He died. They think he was killed. The body was just found the other day."

"He killed the doctor...I'm going to be a bloody millionaire!" the doctor guffawed.

"What?" said Karen, confused.

"Nothing...shut up," giggled the doctor, nervously. "Um, yes, that's very sad to hear. He was an excellent doctor." He paused for a moment before shooing Karen out of the car. "Well, don't let me keep you from whatever it is you do in your free time. Off, you toddle. Thanks for this," he added.

"No problem," she said, getting out of the car. The window was still rolled down and after she stood up she put her hands on the window sill and leaned in. "Be careful. I didn't see it before, but he seems really scary." She walked back toward the house as the doctor lecherously watched her hips sway back and forth.

If Spencer had killed his former doctor, and these session recordings proved anything, this would be just what was needed to make his case. Unable to wait until he was all the way home, the doctor decided to stop off at the office on the way and have a look at the contents of the drive. It was just a few minutes away by car and he could practically see the words of his book writing themselves in his mind. This was going to make him rich! He started drumming on the steering wheel in excitement. "Why yes, Graham Norton, I'd love to come on my show and talk about my book!" he exclaimed aloud to himself, dreaming about an appearance on his favorite chat show. He was glad he only needed to go to the office, as the medicine Nancy had given him was starting to kick in. It could be the combination of the pills with the alcohol from Linnea's all those hours before, but his vision began to go a bit blurry on the outsides of his eyes.

Minutes later, he reached the deserted office. It being Christmas, not a soul was near the building, just a lonely, dark office park. The doctor, of course, had his own set of keys, so he let himself in and bounded up the gray and brown stairwell up to his second floor office. He briskly entered his office and put his keys and phone down on the coffee table on the way to the desk. He sat down in his leather office chair, booted up his laptop, and inserted the drive. Instantly, he was confronted with dozens of video files to choose from. He had to squint to read the screen as his head started to feel heavy from the drugs. He thought he would spend the night here, just to be safe. He could barely make out the file names of the video on the screen, so he began with the first one, which happened to be the most recent date, Spencer's last session with Doctor Michaelson, July 6. He double-clicked and the video opened, beginning to play.

The video depicted Spencer in a gray room, not unlike the office the doctor sat in at that very moment. Spencer was wearing a black hooded sweatshirt and sitting on a brown leather couch. Above him, a brown and yellow, earth-toned painting was hung on the wall, and the table beside him held a clock. This was certainly a therapist's office, thought the doctor; it was sparsely decorated. A voice from off-screen was asking Spencer questions about his dreams and his life. It was similar material that he and Spencer had discussed in their sessions and Doctor Black picked up on that right away. He then clicked through the scrubber bar before finding a part toward the end that caught his eye and stopped his hand. The movement was swift in the video and showed Spencer getting up from the couch and moving off-screen. The doctor rewound a few seconds to see the exchange that preceded this. The off-camera voice, whom he assumed to be Doctor Michaelson, started by asking Spencer, "So are they dreams?"

"They certainly feel like dreams," Spencer shot back.

"But these things really happen," said Michaelson, stoically. "Every time you tell me about a dream, someone really dies."

Spencer adjusted himself in his chair and took a deep breath before continuing. "Are you saying that, that I killed them?"

"Do you kill them?" Michaelson asked, pointedly.

"How could you ask me that?" scoffed Spencer. "You think I kill these people?" He began to get more enraged, standing up and leaving the frame of the camera. "You think I kill these fucking people?!" He shouted at Doctor Michaelson, lunging toward him before the video feed cut out. This was it. This was the smoking gun.

Michaelson turning up dead, the motive, the means, the opportunity all pointing to Spencer, and here was a tape showing his rage toward the doctor. Doctor Black's hair stood on end, pulling itself away from his goosebumped skin. His brain swelled with both the pills and his emotions. While he felt the joy that he was vindicated in his accusations of Spencer, as well as having his career saved, he also felt a fear that if Spencer was onto him, or knew that he had this information, he might be the next casualty. He felt some security in the fact that Spencer had saved his life once, perhaps he was safe now for some unknown reason. He noticed that of all the feelings he had, one feeling that was absent was the pain in his stomach. The anxious knotting of his insides had subsided; he felt free. He also knew that he needed to warn Nancy. If Spencer was in fact dangerous, he might snap and take it out on her, and he could not let that happen to so wonderful a doctor, or so beautiful a woman.

He rose from his chair and started across the room toward the coffee table to retrieve his phone. As he came around his desk, he tripped over the leg, stumbling over the coffee table and landing face-first on the carpet. He slowly picked himself back up, but felt unsteady on his feet. He knew he would need to spend the night here at the office; he had no ability to drive at this point. Then, in the morning, he would bring this video to the local police. He leaned back down to pick up his phone that he had dropped, his back now facing the door. He heard a faint rustling sound coming from the hallway and stood up abruptly, ignoring his phone. He stumbled toward the door to his office to see if he could locate the source of the noise. He looked out into the hallway and across to Karen's empty desk. Nothing. His body relaxed as he turned back into his office and lumbered toward the couch. He plopped down and sleepily rolled his head back, laughing to himself that his mind must be playing tricks on him after watching some of the movies Spencer was so into these past weeks.

Suddenly, in his peripheral vision, a shadow appeared and everything went black. He felt cloth rubbing against his face and a string tightening around his neck. Something pricked him in the shoulder and a few seconds later, he lost consciousness.

# XIII
## IT Is The End

The first voice Doctor Black heard when he woke up was Spencer's. "What the fuck is going on, Doctor?!" he shouted. The doctor had just sleepily raised his head and began to blink his eyes. He needed little adjustment because the room that they were both in was dimly lit and mostly cast in shadow. His nose immediately picked up a damp and musty smell and he felt the wooden planks of what seemed like an old mining cart beneath him.

As he looked around, he determined that they were in what had to be an abandoned carnival or circus. He spotted a faded red and yellow, vintage sign declaring "Wasilewski, Salazar & Schaub's House of Fun - Now Open!" hanging over the entrance to a tunnel just a few yards in front of him. He looked down and saw that his hands were cuffed to a steel bar that ran across the cart, and he became aware that he was strapped into some sort of conveyance that ran on a track. He reasoned that, rather than a coal mining cart, it must be a car for an amusement park ride.

Having not received an answer, Spencer repeated his question, "What is going on here?"

"Wha...well, I...I should be asking you that," stammered the doctor, fearing for his life.

"How the hell should I know?!" shot back Spencer, annoyance in his voice.

The doctor continued to look around the makeshift prison that he and Spencer found himself in. Turning over his right shoulder and craning his neck he could see they had a third in their cell. Nancy was present as well, her arms tied above her as she hung from a wooden beam, her white blouse torn open revealing a black bra. She was unconscious, and her hair draped partially over her face as her head drooped down.

As he looked around, the doctor managed to stammer a response to Spencer. "Wait, you're not the one doing this? I mean, the murders, the killings, it all adds up!" He was becoming more panicked by the second. The doctor was able to get a better look at Spencer, who wore a black hoodie with the word "Kleaver" on the left lapel. His hands were cuffed above his head in two black manacles that hung over the beam above him. His wrists glowed red from struggling to release himself.

"I'm chained to a goddamn wall right now, does it look like I'm in a comfortable position?" asked Spencer, incredulously. "And what are you talking about? What murders?"

"From our sessions! Your dreams," responded the doctor. "Every time you told me about a dream, somebody would die in the real world, in the exact same way. And in the exact same 'where' and 'when' as you happened to be on tour at the time too. If not you, then who?"

"Oh, I don't know, the hundreds of fans that follow us from show to show every tour that we do?" asked Spencer, sarcastically. "Get your head out of your ass!"

"But...but, the murders," stammered the doctor. "They were all in precisely the same manner as—"

"Precisely the same way as what?" interrupted Spencer. "The famous horror movies that I based the last album on? And that our fans are obsessed with?"

"How should *I* know that? I don't go for that rot."

"Well a lot of people do. And we built our career on that rot," snapped Spencer. "But if it's not me, then who the fuck is it?"

"There was that hooded figure."

"What?"

"Back in the fall, when I was outside your apartment. When you caught me, admittedly, and then I followed you to the bar. At the time I thought nothing of it—"

"And you didn't tell the police any of this?" said Spencer, digging for more information. The doctor shook his head no in response. "Oh, great. Now we're going to die. Well, you're going to die, and I'm going to get *Misery*-ed."

"Miseried?" asked the doctor, not following at all.

"*Misery*! It's a book and a movie? I'm surprised you don't know it," commented Spencer. "I've been kidnapped by a crazed fan. You've gotten me *Misery*-ed you son of a bitch!

"I didn't go to the police because I wanted to keep you out of it. And then, I wouldn't be able to keep studying you. For my book..." he trailed off at the end, realizing he had said too much.

"Thanks a million—" started Spencer. He was cut off as the loud popping sound of an electrical arc making connection echoed through the tunnel in front of them. One second later, lights illuminated the "House of Fun" sign over the tunnel entrance, their buzzing sound cutting through what had previously been silence. The buzzing was quickly drowned out by creaky speakers that emanated classic carnival music throughout the chamber they occupied and the tunnel before them.

"What was that?" asked the doctor, looking toward Spencer for any possible answer, perhaps from one of his films.

"I already told you. I don't...knowwwww!" Spencer's voice trailed off as a moveable part of the wall behind him spun around, sending him behind it and out of view. In the location where he had been tied up, an identical wall now stood, missing its prisoner.

"Spencer!" the doctor yelled, seeing if he was just beyond the wall. Panicked, he then turned his head every which way he could, searching for answers in any corner of the room that might hold them. He remembered Nancy behind him. He had to wake her up. "Nancy!" he screamed. But it was no use. She remained out cold. "Nancy! Wake up!" he continued. "Spencer?!"

The conveyance that Doctor Black was sitting in began to move forward. It was still operable and on its track. He was flung toward the tunnel and into an unknown darkness that he feared more than the room he was just sitting in. At least in that main room he had not been alone. Now, however, he had no one else to rely on, or to commiserate with, or even to confide in; he was forced to face whomever was behind this by himself.

After careening through the dark for a few seconds, the cart began to slow. He remained in darkness for what felt like an eternity when finally video screens lit up on the walls of the abandoned shaft. First they were empty and black but slightly illuminating the otherwise pitch-black tunnel. Shortly after the screens turned on, the doctor was greeted by the large face of a clown, projected on the walls over and over again. The face was scary in itself, with bright white makeup, but a twisted smile composed of its black-painted lips furthered the doctor's uneasy feeling. Aside from the white makeup, the clown had a red painted nose and black lines forming the high arches of the eyebrows, as well as lines drawn vertically through its eyes. He was immediately reminded of the white face of the man who had saved him, although this face was far more sinister in its appearance. Orange-gray hair sprung out from the sides of the head behind the smiling face and a white-painted bald spot emerged on top. The face's smile grew bigger and the doctor finally recognized who he was looking at. Here on the screen in front of him, in full clown makeup, was a face that he had just left in the other room. It was Spencer. Despite all of his protestations in the adjacent room, Spencer was behind this. He was behind the scenes, behind the mask, behind the killings. The doctor knew it, but also knew that he may never get out alive. He had little time to begin fearing the worst that may befall him, as soon after he recognized Spencer, the face started to speak.

"Allow me to introduce myself...." he began, the voice unmistakable Spencer's. "But first, a little background. Music please!"

Waltz-like circus music began to swell through the tunnel and the doctor was again propelled forward. After flying through a dark passage he emerged in an open space, much larger than the room in which he first found himself. Before him lay a wooden stage painted black and raised just a few feet off the ground. There were steps on the stage leading up to a platform that held a drum set. Wood framework and stone made the backdrop as well as a makeshift white banner with red letters painted on, spelling out "Doctor Ian Black's All Dead Rock Show."

Spencer appeared in his full clown makeup and a ruffled white clown suit complete with red trim and comically large black buttons, as well as white gloves over his hands. The brown clown shoes on Spencer's feet began to move as he danced to the tempo of the waltz. Four other costumed individuals joined him on the stage. A figure wearing a black tuxedo with a red bowtie and white face paint with red swirls on his cheeks first moved to a chair behind the drums. Two others entered with guitars right after, one in a yellow raincoat and another in a leather apron that appeared to be made of disfigured body parts. Finally, a bass guitar was picked up and strapped on by a man dressed exactly as Spencer had been behind the bar, leather coat and white face paint with black lines.

The jovial music gave way to something louder, more raucous, and the doctor looked on with a mixture of fear and awe.

Spencer picked up a microphone from a stand on the stage-left side, and brought it to the center. He began to sing. A mixture of carnival music and metal, the song also featured brass horns played by two individuals who stood to the side of the stage, both dressed in clown costumes. The doctor was transfixed. Behind the band, a video screen lit up, depicting Spencer in the various costumes that were exactly the outfits he described the figures in his dreams to be wearing. The doctor watched as the videos showed Spencer killing his victims, each scene reminding him of a different dream that Spencer had recounted to him. They were real and they were filmed. This was proof, but proof that he knew would never see the light of day. A fact that he lamented to himself as he watched the horrors of innocent people being savagely slaughtered.

The music continued and the doctor was once again whisked away, handcuffed to his cart. He next entered a large, round stone-lined room that looked like the inside of a cave. It was illuminated by the orange light of torches and had a large banner reading "Come See Buddy Will Jr.'s Freak Show!" The room was otherwise empty except for a large wheel painted with a red and white striped bullseye pattern, which held the unconscious body of Nancy.

From behind the wheel, Spencer soon emerged, sauntering toward the doctor. Slowly, he pulled off the bald cap with the orange hair surrounding it, revealing his natural black hair, still slicked back, as usual. He then removed each of his white gloves and tossed them on the ground. He walked slowly toward the doctor who slouched down in his amusement park cart, defeated.

The doctor started to cry, "It was you. All along it was you." Spencer continued toward him, smiling sadistically at the accusation. "You and your band."

"You know, a good band is hard to find," quipped Spencer. "It took a little while, but I think we finally got the right configuration of total psychotics. Give 'em a bunch of black hoodies and it makes you feel like an army is coming for you. Huh, Doc. But they only assisted in some of the elements. The real dirty work, that was all me."

The doctor's mind replayed the images he had just seen, the video footage of the killings. "You're a monster!" he shouted. "Why are you doing this to me?"

"Fancy Ivy League diploma and you still can't figure it out, can you, Doctor?" replied Spencer, his hands reaching toward the doctor and resting on the top edge of the cart. He leaned forward before pushing himself off and away from Doctor Black, who shook his head no. "I guess my motives aren't as convoluted as John Wayne Gacy's or Charles Manson's," continued Spencer, taking in the room and stretching out his arms as he spoke. He then moved back toward the doctor, leaning down so that he was within breathing distance of him, "It's just good old fashioned revenge." The doctor was now face-to-face with Spencer, their noses just inches away from each other.

"I haven't done anything to you!" pleaded the doctor. "I tried to help you!"

"The hell you did!" snapped Spencer. "You tried to study me. All in the hopes of getting some bullshit book deal. *You* don't give a shit about your patients. And your negligence ruined my fucking life." Spencer straightened back up and began to walk away from the doctor.

"But…we only just met! Ruined how?" the doctor begged.

Spencer paused for a moment to look at the unconscious body of Nancy on the wheel before turning back toward the doctor. "Who do you think killed my sister?" he posited, returning to the edge of the cart and leaning back down toward the doctor's face. "Or my parents, huh? I'm an orphan, remember?"

"But...I thought you killed them," he blurted out.

"Of course not," sneered Spencer. "I was nine years old. What are you? Crazy? But I bet you do remember Floyd Schecter."

The doctor thought for a moment, and then remembered his first patient. It was October of 1994, he was just completing his residency at Harvard and preparing to set up a practice of his own in a town just to the north of Boston. Having studied serial killers and mass murderers throughout his time at Oxford, and now Harvard, he had established a relationship with the nearby Hawshank Prison, where he had done much of his doctoral work. His first case where he would be operating on his own, that is, without a faculty advisor, was that of Floyd Schecter. He would be testifying on the patient's behalf at a dangerousness hearing. He remembered that there was some tension between him and the parole board member, Beverly Marsh, who presided over the hearing. They argued over the use of the term "patient" versus "prisoner." Ms. Marsh also did not seem to bother with whether or not Doctor Black was yet a licensed doctor; she only wanted a simple yes or no answer as to whether or not the patient, prisoner as she called him, would offend again. The doctor remembered believing that this patient, Floyd Schecter, was *in compos mentis,* and thus, having served his time, was eligible to be released from prison and into the world rather than to a mental asylum for an indeterminate amount of time. He certainly was not able to see the future but felt that Floyd was a completely sane person, and the doctor said as much in that hearing. Thinking back, there was something of Spencer that reminded him of Floyd, a darkness in his eyes. Aside from the last realization, he recounted the story aloud for Spencer, who listened patiently while the doctor told him what he already knew about Floyd Schecter and his connection to Doctor Black.

Spencer produced a piece of paper from inside the pocket of his clown pants and held it to the doctor's face. The doctor could see it was the exact report that he had signed those many years prior, declaring Floyd to be sane. "That completely *sane* person," hissed Spencer, "slit my sister's throat wide open and butchered all of her friends. Then he waited for my parents to come home so he could finish the job. I hid for hours under that staircase. Hoping and praying that he wouldn't find me," as he spoke Spencer held back a tear. He took a breath and then asked, "Ring a bell?"

It did. It was the case from Salem where the only survivor was a young boy that he uncovered when researching Spencer's dream. "It wasn't my fault," the doctor blubbered. "How was I supposed to know—"

"How would you have known!?" interrupted Spencer. He paced around the room and then again approached the doctor. "If you had done your job! But that's the problem, Doctor. You see your patients as walking, talking, troubled ATMs. Not real people."

"But you killed real people!" the doctor rebuked.

"And that's all because of you," retorted Spencer. "Floyd Schecter. He was my first. But you, you won't be my last." He turned away from the doctor and started to walk away.

"What about the others?" shouted the doctor, calling after Spencer. "What about Nancy? She had no part in this."

"Didn't she though? Let's see what she says. Oh Nancy, come out come out wherever you are!" Then making a full display of seeing the wheel. "Oh boy, Doc. Looks like she's right here. Right in front of our eyes this entire time. Hello, gorgeous."

Nancy lifted her head and looked at Spencer. "Spencer? Did it work? Did Ian laugh? Why don't I remember?" She then looked toward the doctor. "Ian? There you are. What's happening?" Her hands were tied at forty-five degree angles above her head and her feet splayed out the same way below. Immediately after she spoke, she started to spin, causing her to scream.

"Were you in on this?" whispered the doctor, fearing her betrayal.

"Yes, to an extent. But this wasn't part of it!" she yelled as she turned clockwise on the wheel, slowly at first but now at a much faster pace.

"Nancy here decided to trust me on the fact that I felt you needed a little fun in your life," chortled Spencer. "Is she right, doctor? Do you need a little fun? How about we play a little game?" Spencer produced a set of throwing knives from behind the wheel, holding them up so that the lights of the torches surrounding the chamber reflected off of them.

"Spencer? What are you doing?" yelled Nancy.

"Funny thing about letting someone strap you to a wheel so that they can throw knives at you: it requires a lot of trust. Something that you should never put in other people."

"Spencer!" asked Nancy, concerned. "Spencer, get me off of this thing!" Ignoring her, Spencer walked around to the back of the wheel. "Ian!? Ian help!" she screamed, realizing what was now occurring.

"What did you do to me, Nancy?!" the doctor shouted. "You betrayed me!"

Nancy started spinning faster on the giant "wheel of death," as it is often known. Thinking that he could do little to save her, and perhaps, should do little to save her after she betrayed him, Doctor Black shut Nancy out by closing his eyes. A moment later, he had a change of heart. He wished he could do something and felt it best to reopen his eyes and at least try to forgive her before she died. As soon as he opened his eyes, he met her gaze.

Nancy's eyes immediately widened. The doctor looked down just in time to see her stomach rip open and blood gush outward toward him. Nancy was just barely far enough away from him that he did not get splattered on, but it came close to hitting his cart. Following the blood, the tip of a blade stuck out through her entrails. Nancy gurgled a moment, a look of pleading for her life in her eyes, and then, nothing. She fell limp.

"Nancy!" cried the doctor, quickly repenting his decision to disavow himself of her.

Spencer emerged from behind the wheel of death holding a machete. He tossed the knife to the ground. And then continued. "I bet you thought I was going to throw knives at her, huh? Well, sorry to disappoint you, Doctor, but I've never been too good of a shot."

"How could you do that? Didn't she help you?"

"Helped? Hurt? Who's to say?" Spencer responded. "Red is her color, don't you think?" he asked, admiring her like a piece of art hanging on the wall. "Red coat, red car, maybe even a red herring."

"What do you mean?" asked the doctor.

"She didn't have anything to do with this. All she wanted to do was to help you. She thought I was planning something fun for you. Five years of loyalty, working side by side, and you were ready to throw it all away in an instant."

"So, she was innocent?" the doctor responded.

"Innocent?" he chuckled. "Is anyone truly innocent, doctor? Didn't he who made the lamb make me? Sometimes the blood seeps into your soul. I mean, does anyone fault the tiger for killing the fawn?!"

"She didn't have to die. And now…now you're going to kill me?" queried the doctor, afraid of the answer that might seal his fate.

"No," said Spencer, shaking his head. "I did that hours ago. See that funny feeling? In your eyes, Doctor? That's the tetrodotoxin.

I'm not gonna pull back the final curtain until I'm sure that you're not going to escape and you're not going to survive." The doctor cowered in fear as Spencer continued. "When I woke you up, you had thirty minutes to live....about thirty minutes ago." He smiled.

"What are you going to do now?" mumbled the doctor, his body losing its functional abilities as if right on cue.

"Let's clean up," said Spencer, producing a roll of paper towels from beside him in the cave like a sadistic prop comic. "Then we'll see. But for you, Doctor, it is the end."

The doctor's vision blurred, he reeled from side to side. Finally, he fell toward his right and slumped into the cart. His body seized its last attempt at life. Then he was gone.

# Afterword

It seems natural to address the elephant in the room that remains in this story: mistakes were made in the news coverage of the preceding events. Many of the facts surrounding this case remained unknown until long after the events had occurred—some even remained unreported until the publishing of this book. As a member of the media, I always try to adhere to the facts and report as accurately as possible. And so it is with great apology and a sense of atonement that I now admit to you the errors that were made in this case. Yes, even I, Roy Merkin, was duped by Spencer up until this point, a fact that was evident in my reporting around the time. The news coverage is out there, and I'm sure the clips can be easily found on the internet, but allow me to briefly lay out what we knew then versus now.

At the time of these events, it was believed that Doctor Ian Black's death had occurred as part of a murder-suicide. He was found in the basement of the home of his colleague, Doctor Nancy Price, alongside her body, which had been stabbed through the stomach and mutilated. The basement itself connected into a series of tunnels that ran underground across the town, eventually ending in an abandoned amusement park nearby. The cause of death for Doctor Black was ruled to be poisoning and later thought to be self-administered. Forensic DNA would later link him to a string of murders across the southwestern United States, as well as to several killings in the New England area and Texas. We thought we had found our man, and what a perfect story it was: Serial Killer-Studying Doctor Kills Serially, Ending with Himself. These findings, of course, were entirely mistaken.

During one of the last news reports that I gave on the subject, I wished Spencer well in the hospital. He had also been found in the basement, and claimed the doctor had tried to kill him, but had ultimately failed. Based on what we later learned, I regret having done this. Spencer was taken to the hospital out of precaution so that he may be monitored and his wounds may heal. It seemed, at that moment, that the primary threat, Doctor Black, was subdued. However, nothing could have been further from the truth.

While in the hospital, Spencer used a cell phone to make a series of threatening calls to the nurse at the front desk before killing her. This phone was later traced back to a series of phone calls made to one Sarah Becker three years prior. Sarah was later found brutally murdered and hanging from a tree; no suspects had ever been determined. Those phone records, along with the fact that Spencer had been in the location of many of the murders originally attributed to Doctor Black, actually led a diligent, dedicated, and soon to be decorated Salem police officer named Dewey Riley to crack the case of his lifetime. From there, it was as simple as dominos falling into place. A fire in Doctor Black's office made it difficult to obtain records, but what eventually cracked the case was finding a cloud-backup of all of his files mysteriously sent to Colin Barlow, his former classmate and presumed nemesis. It seemed the doctor had been attempting to pass Spencer off to Colin Barlow, perhaps as an attempt to distance himself from his murderous patient. The attempt, however, was never realized, as the doctor met his final demise. Fittingly, this was at the hands of the very patient he was attempting to transfer.

Spencer is now facing a litany of charges and is set to be tried in a Massachusetts federal court in what looks to be a trial fit for Hollywood—straight out of the movies. It is, however, a very real trial that may further shed some light on whether or not violent film culture caused his movie-freak mind to lose its reality button. On behalf of the entire media circus surrounding this trial, I have a message for our homicidal friend. While we may be watching from the safety of our screens, this trial, and its consequences, will continue to be your reality for years to come:

**"Say goodbye to the Silver Scream, Spencer.**
**Welcome to Horrorwood..."**